Nine by Three: Stories

Nine by Three:
Stories

by Beverly Conner
Hans Ostrom
and Ann Putnam

foreword by
Ronald R. Thomas

Several of these stories have appeared in periodicals, sometimes in slightly different form. The authors are grateful to the editors and readers of *Arches*, *Ploughshares*, *Puget Soundings*, *South Dakota Review*, and *Webster Review*.

Book Design: Sara McIntyre
Copy Editor: Hannah Stephenson
Cover Art: *Three Children by the Lake Dream of their Father*, encaustic painting by Courtney E. Putnam
Authors' Photo: Ross Mulhausen
Collins Press: Jane Carlin

Proceeds from the sale of *Nine By Three* support Collins Library at the University of Puget Sound, Tacoma, WA 98416 USA.

These stories are works of fiction. Any possible similarity between them and actual persons or situations is entirely coincidental.

ISBN-13 978-0-9844175-2-0
ISBN-10 0-9844175-2-4

First Edition

Contents

Foreword

Nine by Three could describe the dimensions of one of those long narrow carpets we call a runner and place in the hallway that leads us from one room to another. These nine stories from three very different writers are like that. Together, Beverly Conner, Hans Ostrom, and Ann Putnam offer a neatly woven fabric – and a hauntingly beautiful one – that carries us down the corridors connecting the rooms of our experience of childhood and adulthood, mourning and recovery, winter and spring. As these narratives reveal, some of these journeys are long, some come all too suddenly, and some never end. Each story in the sequence springs from a dislocating and disorienting event and then stitches together a set of experiences to offer a touching account of something lost and something else found, conveying us from a place we must abandon to another into which we must enter.

For Hans Ostrom, whose "My Last Days in the Solar System" opens the volume, the journey begins with a childhood memory: the most unfortunate fall of a second-grader, whose precociousness provokes his forced transfer from the imaginary realm of an ideal elementary school classroom to the unfriendly confines of the upper school. "Handled like a prisoner exchange except no one was coming over from the other side," the promotion is experienced by the young scholar as a tragic descent: from soaring in the imagined glory of the solar system on the wall to hostile confinement within alien planet earth's profane cruelty and banality. Through the eyes of Ostrom's characters we witness other falls from grace that call out for redemption and relocation, from the familiar streets of Tacoma to the faraway shadows of Kenya's jungles. They each follow the corridors of their dreams and delusions, reach out to the savannahs of fear and awe, and are haunted by the prophecies of everything from a green bird singing to the mysterious divinity of a white rhinoceros on the loose. All of these characters are living, at once, in and out of this world.

The first of Beverly Conner's stories also emerges from a searing childhood memory: the trauma of surviving the undertow from an irresistible riptide, then negotiating the blinding confusion of the Santa Ana winds, and, finally, losing a parent to the imagined enemies of a generation caught "in the hesitation between two breaths." Each of Conner's three tales traces another individual's painful attempt at recovery from a profound and irreplaceable loss – of a parent, a partner, a child – and goes on to explore the often inadequate mechanisms of coping we employ to either run away, fill the void, or rise above it. It is hard to swim against the current, as these stories show, and there are times when the only option left is to let it carry you away for a while.

And then, there is "The Bear." Set in a place called "Swift Current" on a camping trip in Montana's Glacier National Park, Ann Putnam's first story begins with the reassuring words of a parent to her anxious children that the bear that has recently been reported invading other campsites "is dead... so there isn't anything to worry about anymore." But this landscape is haunted by other shadows, too, and by deeper currents of fear and memory: notably, by the narrator's recollection of her first encounter with a grizzly, and of her beloved grandfather who, with "large hands like paws," long ago guided her through the wilderness of her childhood entry into nature. Putnam's stories are encounters with the specters of ancient and modern fears and all the things there are still to worry about: from a departed ancestor to a partner's deadly cancer to a pet dog's funeral. Each is accompanied by "the sound of absence everywhere" and the competing tones of a fragile contingency alternating with fierce resolution. The grizzly is never quite dead or gone.

The final story, Putnam's "Divination," finishes the volume with a perfectly mysterious benediction upon the losses (and gains) of all the stories in *Nine by Three*. Like the sacrificial rite conducted in an unknown tongue in this story, the entire collection is an act of recovery, a rhythmic ritual of transference, and an undying determination to find one's way home. *Nine by Three* forms the bridge to bring us back, weaves a carpet – in many dimensions – that lines our lonely corridors and leads us from the familiar rooms of our everyday habitation to the darker places up ahead in which we have not yet made ourselves at home. These stories extend a warm invitation to walk on with them.

Ronald R. Thomas
March 20, 2011

My Last Days In The Solar System

Hans Ostrom

I

My last days in the solar system were spent in a canyon of California's Sierra Nevada mountains. Claytonville was the place.

I was seven years old and in the second grade, which was presided over by Mrs. Franz – Vera Franz. None of us seven-year-olds ever thought of her as "Vera," much less call her by that name. In fact, years later, when I heard my mother refer to Mrs. Franz as Vera, I was shocked – by the utterance, by the intimacy a first name suggests, by the whole different life for Mrs. Franz beyond Claytonville School that *Vera* implied.

Claytonville School sat on a hill, was built in a rectangle with one end open, and consisted of two short halls containing three classrooms each. One set of classrooms was reserved for grades 1 through 8, another for high school. By now you've inferred the population of Claytonville was in the low hundreds.

Where the two halls were conjoined by a short corridor, the principal's office and the teachers' room were situated.

The teachers' room was always filled with cigarette smoke, the principal's office always with the principal.

Mr. McGuire. He was large and had a red face decorated with a red nose. He wore navy blue suits and black wing-tipped shoes that pounded the hard floors of the school like a jackhammer.

When Mr. McGuire was on the playground, you could, if you were a moderately alert child, observe his coughing and bringing something up from his lungs through his throat into his mouth, and then you could witness his spitting the substance like a yellow bullet into rocky dirt. If you walked near him as everyone returned from recess to the building, you could hear his shoes grind grit on the asphalt of the hill.

Mrs. Franz's room was the first of three on the corridor reserved for grades 1 through 8. It held the first and second grades, which added up to fifteen students, at most, in any given year. The students were the daughters and sons of loggers, laborers, miners, forest-rangers, fry-cooks, waitresses, saloon-owners, and so on.

Mrs. Franz kept the room immaculate, the desks in perfect rows, the beige tile floor waxed and shiny, the cork bulletin-boards and the green chalkboard pristine.

Members of grades one and two faced each other like wee armies, with a demilitarized zone between us.

For reading, writing, and arithmetic, we were separate classes. Mrs. Franz would start one grade on an activity, and as students busied themselves, heads bent, tongues lolled out like those of dogs, she'd move to the other grade and get them started on something. By that time, of course, at least one member of the other grade would have become antsy, mischievous, or even wanton.

Reprisal was swift but never rushed. Mrs. Franz would return to that side of the room, unperturbed but purposeful. She took action. It might consist of a tap on the shoulder. Perhaps a deft pinch of one ear, never enough to cause physical pain. Sometimes only a look, sometimes just speaking the person's name: "Ian." Or "Kathy." Once she said my name like that because I was making too much noise. "Jake," she said. I was mortified.

Sometimes Mrs. Franz merely stood beside the outlaw in question like a shadow of enormous potentiality or a cloud capable of raining punishment. In any case, order – busy, productive order – returned. She scared us.

For some activities, we were one group. To study music we would sing in rounds or scrape and knock wooden blocks together to an evasive rhythm. To explore the subject of hygiene, we were instructed by Mrs. Franz on how to brush our teeth and how to wash our faces with a cloth. In preparation for holidays, we tortured coarse paper with milky glue and dull scissors. Our curriculum was earth-bound.

Through it all, Mrs. Franz remained unflustered, unflappable, calm, firm, and frightening. *Vera Franz* was quite a different sort of person. More about that soon.

Mrs. Franz was slender and fit, with good balance and perfect posture. My memory of her wardrobe includes cotton print dresses, not loud but also not drab. In winter she wore a dark blue wool overcoat to school. Her hair was black with streaks of gray – wavy; cut fairly short. Her eyes were dark blue, her mouth firm. She wore little makeup – lipstick, certainly, and maybe the slightest dash of rouge.

Now that I think of it, she probably would have trimmed her eyebrows but not have plucked them. She tucked delicate, lace-bordered handkerchiefs into the sleeve of her dresses.

At some point in her life, Mrs. Franz had turned forty. This might have happened when she was thirty or when she was fifty. In any case, she was forty when she taught me, and she remained forty for several years after that.

But what of me, and what of the solar system? Such pressing questions.

By the time I entered the second grade, I'd become exceptional, but I recognize you don't need assistance to gauge the relativity of the term, particularly as it was deployed in a remote canyon of the Sierra Nevada.

I was a Very Good Boy, for one thing, and for another, because of my mother's belief that education begins at home, I was already a trained reader. I devoured every scrap of print Mrs. Franz assigned. Writing and arithmetic came easily to me, too. I willed myself to make my eccentric printing and cursive conform to Mrs. Franz's standards, chiefly because I didn't want to disappoint her. In any event, I strode like a giant across the world of second grade.

Like all exceptions, I became a problem. I sensed it myself. Because I was quicker than my classmates, I either dominated activities or finished them much too quickly. Occasionally – and ineffectually – I'd try to pretend to be slower than I was. If we were reading alone, I'd walk up to Mrs. Franz's desk and pretend to ask her how to pronounce a word. She would look at me, suspicion subtly revealed in her eyes, and say, "I think you know that word, Jake. Say it." And I would say it, pretending to falter. I was such a bad actor and so hungry for praise that I couldn't follow through on the deception. "You see?" Mrs. Franz would say. "You knew it. Very well. Now return to your desk, please."

I had every reason in the solar system to want to remain in second grade forever. I had mastered that world. I was having fun. I had friends, the best of whom was Whistle Kennedy, a Washo Indian boy who lived with white foster parents. Whistle was quiet and clever and a star in his own right – on the playground and in the woods. Moreover, he could belch on command. "Whis," I'd say on the playground, "when Kathy Reardon walks by, burp." And he'd give me a deadpan glance, then with perfect timing belch like a bullfrog precisely when fastidious Kathy came closest. She would scream and run. Our own comedy enthralled us.

In the woods, Whis had what seems now to be not just an uncanny but an otherworldly ability to discover arrowheads. At the time, of course, I and the other boys simply thought that this was one thing one of our friends, Whis, did. Indeed, Whis had the same attitude toward his and others' special abilities. Robert could stand on his head expertly, Ian knew how to throw a knife so it stuck in wood, I knew how to pronounce difficult words and negotiate with hound-dogs, Stan knew how to gather useful intelligence about girls, and Whis knew exactly what was in the woods and precisely where to find it, including arrowheads. All of us had something to contribute.

And so, no, there was no reason to leave second

grade. For me there seemed to be an endless, if carefully dispensed, reservoir of praise from the Smartest Person in the World, Mrs. Franz, age forty. She knew everything I needed to know, I knew I could learn everything she had to teach, and I loved living in the light of her authority.

Most of all, however, and most irrationally of all, I loved the solar system.

It was the one permanent display in Mrs. Franz's room. It took up one whole bulletin board and consisted of a large poster representing the sun and the planets. Space was a deep navy blue, with a ration of stars. The sun was bright but affable, not explosive. It looked more like a light-bulb than a star of nuclear energy. The planets were more or less lined up like pals, although not in the kind of order Mrs. Franz required of her desks. Most planets were blue, green, brown, or red. Saturn, however, was outlandish (so to speak), splashed with several colors. Mars was Christmas red, so much so that I invented a personal myth in which Santa Claus originated from Mars. Pluto was a deep chocolate brown and almost lost in the navy blue of space. Decades later, of course, Pluto would be decommissioned as a planet, a heresy that enraged me.

Because I had so much time on my hands in class, having completed tasks quickly, I'd often stare at the solar system for minutes, which in childhood's Relativity extend far beyond 60 seconds each. I assume my mouth was agape, my eyes glassy. The poster said almost everything to me that I wanted to hear, although I'm still not completely sure what the message was. Something about beautiful colors and endless space – inviting and safe space. Something about the order of spheres, and something about being able to race through what Mrs. Franz had assigned and fly back to the solar system. Something, surely, about solitude and self-love.

Curiously, I did not assume that the Earth in the poster was the Earth I lived on, and in any case, I didn't like the name, "Earth," arguably the most boring name in the solar system, a kind of grunt. To my mind, the solar system was a place elsewhere, unrelated to the planet on which I lived. I was utterly comfortable with this paradox. It really wasn't a paradox. I lived in Claytonville, beside a rapid alpine river, but when I went to school, I could travel to the solar system, of which Claytonville was not a member, but to which Mrs. Franz's classroom was the doorway.

II

When I left the solar system, I didn't know I was leaving it, let alone that I was leaving it forever.

Late in November of my second-grade year, Mrs. Franz apparently ran out of things to assign me. I say "apparently" because I never felt bored. I felt everything was easy, but the feeling was good. Nonetheless, she told the principal (Mr. McGuire) and my parents that I was bored, and she conferred with Mrs. Wiggins, the teacher of grades three through five (in the classroom next door), and all of them decided that I must skip ahead to third grade immediately.

The final decision was made on a bleak, snowy November day. My father, a stone mason, took off from work one morning and came to school with my mother. Mrs. Franz delivered me to Mr. McGuire's office, where my parents and I met with the large principal.

Mr. McGuire was smoking; or rather, a cigarette lay in an amber ashtray and released a languid stream of smoke toward the acoustic-tiled ceiling. His voice was husky, and I thought his hand was huge when it patted me on the shoulder.

As I remember it, my parents were as polite as I. It was the same kind of politeness they showed to people who visited our house for the first time. They seemed stiff and subdued, deferential, but I knew them usually to be anything other than deferential. My father wore clean, well used bluejeans and a black-and-red wool jacket, plaid. He held his cloth hat in his hands. My mother – she would have worn a skirt and nylons, would have gotten up an hour earlier than usual to "get ready" for this meeting.

I recall that my bowels were in turmoil as a result of real fear. More than I realized, there was a part of my mind that knew true change was on its way, big change. I was the subject of the conversation, but I did not join in. I wished Mr. McGuire had a poster of the solar system in his office at which I could stare.

He was insincere, although I don't know whether I would have sensed that then. I remember his tone, mostly: husky, falsely polite, a bit too loud, with an edge of impatience. "I think it's the best, I think he'll be happy, he needs to be challenged...." That's what he was saying. My mother listened hard; to her, education was everything. She took Mr. McGuire more seriously than he took himself, certainly more seriously than he took her.

My father listened intently, too, but a hint of anger soon appeared on his face, one I'd learned to recognize quickly. It was the kind of anger his face showed when, in the morning, he talked to Mother about someone else on the crew with whom he worked – a man who was lazy or who showed up drunk. In any case, in the meeting my father had ceased to be deferential, although he remained reserved. Now I assume he was probably angry at Mr. McGuire, not for suggesting that I should skip grades, but because he'd left a cigarette burning in an ashtray ("Either smoke the goddamned thing or snuff it out, you stupid sonofabitch" is the kind of sentence that would have taken shape in my father's mind), and because McGuire talked too much while imparting too little information. Mr. McGuire was the sort of man my father called a "bull-shitter," and on the list of quasi-criminal character flaws my father kept in his head, few were worse than being a bull-shitter.

Although my mind gathered these details back then, I'm sure in the moment I was focused chiefly on my fear. I probably stared at my shoes or at gray clouds visible through Mr. McGuire's window. The scene ended soon. I'd not spoken. Mother kissed me on the top of my forehead. Father pawed my head like a disinterested bear. They departed. Mr. McGuire escorted me back to Mrs. Franz's room, the click of his wing-tips sounding like a military march.

In the communal consciousness of second grade, to return from the principal's office was to return from Hell, partly because, in those days, principals were allowed to keep and deploy a wooden paddle in their offices. The unwritten rule was that Mr. McGuire was allowed to hit boys with the paddle through the eighth-grade year.

The faces of my classmates in both grades turned toward me uniformly like flowers toward the sun. The hush of the classroom was more extensive than usual. Then came a brief dialogue between Mr. McGuire and Mrs. Franz. Then on Mrs. Franz's face appeared the slightest and most fleeting apologetic glance as she asked me to return to my desk.

In a guarded voice, Whistle Kennedy asked me, "What'd you do, Jake? Kathy says you got in trouble for hitting her in the head with the kick-ball."

At that moment, I felt boundless affection for Whis – for his sincere concern, his loyalty, his gullibility, his round face. I also felt warmth for Kathy Reardon. I don't know why, but I took her lie about the kick-ball as a gesture of kindness. She thought enough of me to invent a criminal record for me. It was touching. Kathy and Whis and I were connected, even if it was through a system of childish cruelty and of personalities in search of form. Apparently, Kathy wanted us to remain connected, for of all the students, she would have been the one to know the truth, which her parents would have picked up from Claytonville gossip. Kathy's reports on what our parents and other adults said and thought were extensive and accurate. She was the one – not I, the alleged wordsmith – who had taught us all what the word "divorce" meant, for example. Yet now she'd chosen to mislead Whis, perhaps to protect his feelings for an hour.

"It wasn't so bad," I said. "He didn't use the paddle."

But at recess, I told him the truth. I told him I was leaving second grade.

"Will we still be pals?" he asked. I think he would have said "pals."

"Yes," I said. We were in the gym because of the snow. I remember wild cacophony, the smell of ancient perspiration and wet clothes, and Whistle's sad face. I remember feeling abandoned even though I was in the context of a crowd and in the presence of a pal.

III

The very next day I left Vera Franz's class. The transfer was handled like a prisoner-exchange, except no one was coming over from the other side. Mrs. Franz escorted me to a point precisely half-way down the corridor, where we were met by Mrs. Wiggins.

Mrs. Wiggins was friendly but harried. Stray wisps of her fine, curly red hair floated toward the ceiling. She was out of breath. She was as plump and disheveled as Mrs. Franz was slender and composed. Mainly I clung to the hopeful fact that Mrs. Wiggins seemed friendly.

Just before the exchange was made, Mrs. Franz said, "Be good, Jake."

I didn't understand her. I didn't take the remark as a fare-thee-well, but as a kind of prophecy – as if, indeed, I weren't going to be good.

"Okay," I said, feeling as if I were telling a lie.

Then came turmoil. Noise. Sheer noise. Chaos. An absence of gravity. In Mrs. Wiggins' classroom, there were too many children with too much unrestricted energy and power, almost as if gravity were on the verge of losing its grip. Desks were out of order. Projectiles filled the air. Spitballs clung to the ceiling. Compartments in desks apparently held caches of rubber bands and paper clips used as weapons. Snot was turned into kinds of bullets. Ears got flicked and hair got pulled. Screams of pain were not unusual, nor were wicked snickers. Beneath the unruliness lay a dry foundation of boredom and aimlessness, however. The chalkboards were smeared, the bulletin boards in disarray, the floor streaked with mud, stacks of books and ceramics and other "projects" in haphazard accumulation.

This, then, was Mrs. Wiggins' classroom, to which I had been sentenced. That day and every day, such was Mrs. Wiggins' room. Most of all, I remember the noise. And on that first day, it was like walking into a cacophonous wall. Expecting to be stared at, I was ignored. The noise simply absorbed me.

The students were ostensibly taking an Achievement Test, which (I later learned) resulted in the identification of one's IQ, or so was the theory. Probably the taking of the Achievement Test was the reason I was transferred that day. When, finally, Mrs. Wiggins was able to subdue the students, she told us to "TURN TO THE NEXT PAGE" or to "STOP: DO NOT GO BEYOND THIS PAGE." I'd read these directions already, and I did not understand why Mrs. Wiggins was repeating them in a voice that badly attempted to represent capital letters. We filled in bubbles on stiff cards, which I assume were then eaten and digested by room-size computers in Sacramento.

Intuitively, I knew the group I had entered was composed chiefly of criminals and their victims, and my three years in that prison only enlarged upon my instincts. Noise was always to reign, except for rare moments – let's say three times per semester – when Mrs. Wiggins, distraught at her desk, would scream hideously, and in capital letters,

"LITTLE PEOPLE! LITTLE PEOPLE! DEAR LORD, GIVE ME STRENGTH! LITTLE PEOPLE, SHUT UP! THAT IS NOT A NICE WAY TO PUT IT, BUT YOU MUST SHUT UP!" Often she put the button on this ritualized scene by grabbing a textbook and flinging it against the wall. Then, in the ensuing silence, she would lower her face into her hands and, this time murmuring to herself, say again, "Dear Lord, give me strength."

I continued to do well in school, mostly because my parents identified no other option. Out of stupendous boredom, however, I got behind 27 pages in a workbook by the end of one fall semester. Mrs. Wiggins finally reported the lapse to my parents. Consequently, I spent a good part of Christmas vacation sitting at the kitchen table, catching up on the workbook, under my mother's surveillance, which was reinforced by looks of disapprobation from my father when he marched through the kitchen or sat at the table eating. Additionally, my parents let a variety of aunts, uncles, and cousins know about my workbook-failure. They'd decided I had shame coming to me.

Much of the joy I'd taken from learning in Mrs. Franz's class disappeared in the Wigginsian Realm. The experience was like going backstage during a magician's act and seeing how it all was done. What had been magical had become brute facts: students always on the edge of mutiny; male students wallowing in illusory power before they headed to upper grades and thence to high school and finally into back-breaking work in the canyon or warfare in Viet Nam. Female students negotiated the brute force of the boys. Mrs. Wiggins, overwhelmed, stampeded, became numb to it all. When I saw Kathy Reardon outside of class, she associated me with the rest of the criminals in my classroom and had no time for me. Whistle and I drifted apart, and then one day he was gone – over to the Sierra Valley, it was said, to live with another foster-family and to go to school there. We never saw each other again.

Gradually, I became aware that Mrs. Wiggins' classroom was part of "the real world" my parents and other adults occasionally mentioned. More quickly than gradually, I also inferred that "the real world" was at once a sinister place and yet the only place in which one should aspire to live. The solar system represented by Mrs. Franz's poster became more desirable, by contrast, all the time.

My parents knew Mrs. Wiggins' class was real, and they did not celebrate the fact. They worried about it. After all, the original plan had been to have me skip a grade so I could be challenged, not demoralized. During the Christmas break when I caught up on the workbook, I sensed my mother was as disappointed in Mrs. Wiggins as she was in me. Indeed, I knew she knew the real problem lay with Mrs. Wiggins, and she knew that I knew she mustn't denigrate Mrs. Wiggins in my presence. For those three years I spent in Wiggins World, my parents and I would sometimes enter silent moments in which we listened to but did not speak about our mutual regret.

I knew then and know now not much could have been done to change the situation. Mr. McGuire was a chain-smoking bull-shitter and was satisfied to have a warm body in front of grades three through five. In fairness to him, enticing persons to teach for little pay in a village stuck to the side of a mountain in the High Sierra was no easy task; maybe it's an easier endeavor these days. To keep the situation in further perspective, I must note that I was well fed and sheltered, I learned a few things at Claytonville School, and I got my IQ reported to the State of California. Eventually I matriculated out of Wiggins World and into sixth grade.

IV

It's hard to know exactly what I thought back then about having to leave the solar system, not to mention Mrs. Franz's galaxy. Evidently, I started accepting most of it: the fact that, as a person progressed or was ejected from second grade to third and from there into life-in-general, life-in-general became "the real world," and more is the pity; the fact that Mrs. Wiggins was incompetent; the fact that, if you were more or less a reflective person, you nonetheless had to find a way to live amidst ignorant noise.

I know for sure I did not understand Vera Franz, her situation.

As I got older, of course, I found out more about her life, though her life beyond Claytonville School still remained largely a fiction to me. She was married to Henry Franz, who used to be a ship's mechanic but who then decided to become officially unemployed because of "a bad back," which in Claytonville remained in quotation marks because everyone suspected Henry was simply lazy and cravenly content to rely on his wife for a living.

As early as fifth grade, my last season in Mrs. Wiggins chaotic parlor, I could tell that Mr. Franz was a bull-shitter of the highest order. He knew how to do everything, according to him – from cutting Christmas trees to plumbing a toilet to catching Eastern Brook trout. Except he did none of these things. And he had been everywhere, from Claytonville to Singapore. Except that the number of places he'd visited seemed to increase each year, even though he rarely left Claytonville. Young as I was, I sensed a slight embarrassment on Vera's part that she was married to him, that he was so full of himself, that he didn't work, that all they had was each other, no children.

Once Mrs. Franz paid a visit to Mrs. Wiggins' class. Later I invented an excessive, amorphous analogy between the visit and Christ's having gone into the Wilderness.

Mrs. Franz was there to give a ceramics demonstration. Mrs. Wiggins was an expert in ceramics — the kind you pour into prefabricated molds, allow to dry, paint more or less by numbers, and fire in a portable electric kiln. Out came ashtrays, squirrels, and saucers. Failsafe ceramics.

But Mrs. Franz had taken a summer course in free-form ceramics: just you and the wheel and the clay. She showed us what she had made. Vases of startling shapes, painted wildly. A glazed bowl that asked to be stared at. We were all stunned. Well, at least we were all quietly respectful. I was stunned. I knew instantly there was something real about these creations that made our molded things seem pointless. I knew her work belonged to the real world but not to "the real world"; her work belonged in the solar system.

At any rate, a certain deep logic bubbled up in me. Of course, I thought: out-of-control, distracted Mrs. Wiggins *would* be an expert in prefabricated ceramics, whereas composed Mrs. Franz would be the *artist*.

After school that day, as I meandered down the hill, I saw Mrs. Franz walking toward the car in which her husband waited. Exhaust came out of the rusted tail-pipe. He kept the car running to keep himself warm, even though it was a pleasant spring day. Mrs. Franz, no doubt, counted pennies and watched the gasoline-allowance carefully.

She didn't see me. I was behind her. She was carrying her ceramics in a cardboard box. It was one of the first times in my life that I felt pity, abject pity, for someone I liked. There was simply something sad about her noble posture, about her carrying her art in a cardboard box, and about her having to get into Henry Franz's rusting car. I remember she set the box down on the asphalt, and as she opened the rear door of the car, she tucked a stray curl of hair behind one ear, and to me this gesture made her too vulnerable, and at that moment, she ceased to be the impervious Mrs. Franz I had known. She had become Vera Franz. That day when I got home, I was troubled and moody, and Mother, who connected my moods to the classroom, assumed I had done badly on Mrs. Wiggins' geography test, on which I'd made no errors.

Then, when I was in eighth grade, my last year at Claytonville School, came the following episode.

It was in November again, late one afternoon on one of what we used to call "minimum days." Apparently Mr. McGuire had called a special meeting of teachers, so the students were sent home early. I was one of the last – perhaps *the* last – to leave school because I was trying to finish a science project, something to do with igneous rock.

At about 2:00 p.m., I grabbed my coat, left the classroom, and walked briskly down the corridor. I passed Mrs. Wiggins' door, which was shut – and the lights were out. I stopped and looked through the door's small window. I was witnessing silence in Mrs. Wiggins' classroom. Astonishing. I moved on. When I reached Mrs. Franz's door, I saw that it was open and that the lights were still on, and without thinking, I walked in.

Mrs. Franz sat at a table in the back, head bent, writing. All the children had left. It seemed like a tiny universe, this room, but I was exhilarated to have returned, and to see how clean and bright everything was. Of course, everything also seemed extraordinarily small. Compared to my second-grade self, I was an immense eighth-grader, long-limbed and gawky. I stood there. Mrs. Franz didn't become aware of my presence right away, and I didn't get embarrassed until she looked up, surprised.

"Why, Jake. Hello."

I stammered something about staying late for science and then let my shyness wedge me into a paralytic silence. She came to my assistance.

"Your mother tells me you'll go to high school in Sacramento."

"Yes. I'm going to live with an aunt," I said. "Uh – they have football and theater and everything. More to do." I felt like an ape.

"That will be great," she said. "You deserve to be challenged, Jake."

At that moment, it was obvious that the word "challenged" echoed in both our minds. It took us both back to the day I'd been dispatched from second grade and sent to Wiggins World. "I mean," said Mrs. Franz, "the curriculum will offer many opportunities."

Then I realized I had my back to the solar system. I prayed it would still be there. I turned around, and it was.

It was there. The poster was faded, and it was not very interesting, of course. But part of me could still see it in the old way. I stared at it. I felt Mrs. Franz staring at me, so I turned around.

"You haven't taken it down," I said.

She briefly looked puzzled but then made the connection. "Oh — that. Was that there when you were in here? Perhaps I should take it down. I never do a lesson with it or talk about it. I leave it there just to give them something to look at when they feel they need to look at something."

"I loved looking at it," I said. I accumulated some courage and, without being invited to do so, I sat down at the table next to Vera Franz.

I felt my lips tremble and heard my voice crack, but I got out what I needed to say. "Mrs. Franz, I learned a lot from you. I — I hated leaving here."

She flushed and said, "Oh, Jake." For a moment, I thought she would remain composed, remain Mrs. Franz. But she didn't. She touched my cheek with her hand and said, "Jake, you were such a good student. So bright. Such a joy.... Do well in Sacramento." Her eyes filled with tears, and so did mine, but neither of us let tears escape. Emotion was all right, but at the same time, Vera and I were firmly earthbound.

Then suddenly I understood what she had meant all those years ago during the prisoner-exchange. "Be good," she had said as she released me to Mrs. Wiggins. She had meant "Do well."

Just then Mr. McGuire burst into the room, his wingtips thundering. I gathered my coat and stood up. Mrs.

Franz gathered herself and arose.

McGuire said, “Hello, Jake. You’re here awful late.” Like me, Mrs. Franz probably had the urge to say, “awfully, not awful.” McGuire coughed up something but swallowed it back down. Then he looked hard at Mrs. Franz’s face and said, “Mrs. Franz, are you all right?”

“Yes, Mr. McGuire,” she said. “I’m fine.”

“We’ve been talking about my grandmother,” I lied. “She’s in the hospital dying.”

“Oh,” he said, embarrassed, suddenly powerless, but satisfied with the explanation for why Vera Franz looked to be full of emotion. I scurried past him. By that year, I had no living grandparents, but something had told me McGuire held too much power over Vera Franz and was not above exploiting a crack in her composure – though in what way, I didn't know. The lie came easily to me. I wasn’t being good, but I was doing well: It was in the service of Mrs. Franz.

My parents had done some calculating, had seen how few students from Claytonville went to college and, of the ones who went, how few lasted there. That’s why they sent me to live with an aunt in Sacramento and go to high school there.

In high school I did fine. In football, I played free safety, getting a view of the whole field (in Mrs. Franz’s solar system, Pluto played free safety), getting exposed for all to see when a receiver beat me on a deep route, colliding with halfbacks who’d built up a head of steam, and every so often entering an adrenaline-charged, fleeting moment of something like fame when I intercepted a pass and heard the spectators’ voices roar as one. I played basketball and baseball, too, but I was a mediocre athlete, not least of all because I tended to lose interest. Sometimes I asked myself rhetorically if it mattered whether the Broncos defeated the Cougars on a Friday night that would be devoured almost instantly by the infinite maw of time. Sometimes in the mist of contest, I'd turn and stare at cheerleaders, spectators, rafters, the lights, or the sky.

I acted in *The Crucible* (playing Ezekiel Cheever), fell in love with books again, got figuratively intoxicated by the presence of young women in the real world, got literally intoxicated on beer and slo-gin, and, like other young men my age, saw Viet Nam looming. I went to college and eventually earned more than one degree.

At some point in these years, I learned my instincts about Mr. McGuire's power over Vera were correct. Apparently, Mrs. Franz, the best teacher Claytonville School might ever know, had been working with what's known as a provisional credential, meaning McGuire could have given her the boot any time on any or no pretext, meaning Vera was no doubt in perpetual anxiety about losing her job, on which she and her husband depended. Meanwhile, Mrs. Wiggins sat in the midst of chaotic Wiggins World without the slightest worry about being fired.

I saw Vera Franz exactly once more after our afternoon meeting on that minimum day. I was home from college one summer and ran into her in the Claytonville grocery store. She was old, no longer forty. She had either retired or was about to retire – I don't recall. Her face brightened when she saw me, and I clutched her hand, which was soft and now seemed so small. Although she was old, she didn't look like what used to be called a schoolmarm or a spinster. Hers was a face from which I could still learn everything, I felt, and I wanted to ask her a question about a word I already knew how to pronounce. Instead we exchanged conventional pleasantries, nothing crucial. Henry Franz was still alive and talking and knowing everything, I learned.

I regret not having embraced her then, and I remain guilty – if that's the word – about the look in her eyes: a look that said I'd been one of her brightest students, the context of mere Claytonville notwithstanding. But standing in the grocery store before Mrs. Franz, I didn't know whether I had done well enough or been good enough to have earned the admiration and nostalgia I saw in her eyes.

V

Two years later, Vera Franz was killed in an automobile accident – in Sacramento, of all places. Henry Franz was driving and had turned into oncoming traffic, no doubt imagining he knew everything about left-turn lanes. Vera's side of the car took the mass and velocity. I heard she died instantly, but how can anyone know that for a fact?

When my mother gave me this news over the phone, she gave it the way she reported most news from Claytonville: with a matter-of-factness designed to acknowledge that, as I was now out of the canyon, I could take or leave the news as I pleased. I think I surprised if not shocked her by being struck so hard by the news. First I was subdued. Then sentimentality engulfed me. I don't recall the words I spoke over the phone, but I remember how their force hit my mother so unexpectedly. Then she said, "Vera was your favorite teacher, wasn't she, Jake?" *Vera*. "She was," I said, "yes."

Whistle Kennedy got killed in Viet Nam. His draft-eligibility lottery-number had been just low enough to get him drafted. Moreover, he'd been a year older than I – something I hadn't known in Claytonville. So really he should have left Mrs. Franz's class and gone to Wiggins world, not I. Also, my draft-number was 007, which made for a predictable joke briefly but which also meant the Army would snap me up in a flash. Because I was one year younger than Whis, however, I didn't get drafted, for Nixon suspended the draft. Whistle had been born a Washo Indian, turned into an orphan early, and received lousy education, so those allegedly concerned had held him back a year in school. I'd not been born a Washo Indian or made an orphan, and my parents' concern with education loomed over me like a mountain peak. I'd been born on a different day in a different year from Whistle's day and year. My draft-number was low, but I never had to face the consequences of that or of the real world in Viet Nam. Whistle got shot to death in a swamp; thousands of Americans died there, as well as thousands of Vietnamese – while I'd been allowed to continue living and learning.

Kathy Reardon, whom Whistle had tormented genially with well crafted belches, got married and divorced twice. Both husbands had been abusive. I learned this from Kathy herself when we ran into each other at O'Hare Airport. She was living in Ohio, working for a corporation, and flying back to California to arrange her mother's funeral. I was flying from California to a conference in New York. Our Chicago layovers left time for a couple drinks in an airport bar. We both expressed grief about Mrs. Franz and Whistle, among others.

Kathy's face was beautiful but hard. Her clothes and the stylish cut of her hair betrayed nothing about her having grown up in a hard-scrabble mountain town. She said, "I was so jealous, I mean envious, of you when you skipped out of second grade, but then when I got to Mrs. Wiggins' class the next year, I knew the joke had been on you."

"Indeed," I said.

"Did we become friends?"

"I think we did." I remembered dancing with her once in the gym when we were in 7th grade, but I resisted the temptation to ask her if she remembered. "But," I continued, "you know, both of us were on our way out of Claytonville, so.... Some people our age never left."

"At least two our age got married to each other."

"Incidentally, you were, you are, smarter than I."

"Bullshit."

"No. You beat me in a three-class spelling contest after you came to Wiggins' room, and in math you left me in the dust of asymptotes."

"Who remembers shit like that?" She paused and looked at the small river of people flowing past the bar. "I guess Claytonville never leaves you, I mean us."

"That sounds profound, but what does it mean?"

"I'm a hick, and so are you."

"Yep," I said. "Yep" is a hick-word. Kathy warmed to the topic:

"Sometimes in meetings I just want to say, 'Shut up and do your fucking job. This isn't hard. It's not like felling a tree on a forty-degree slope or hard-rock mining.'

But I don't. I don't say it. I'm fluent in corporatese. I say shit like, "Well, what *I'm* hearing from the group about our objectives is...." Her confession made me feel as if I had to share one.

"I walk slowly in cities. So when I get to New York, I'll saunter, and I'll be like a big dumb boulder in the manic flow."

"And get nudged and shoved and glared at," she said. "Why not walk faster, Jake? Hell, if you did that to me, I'd walk up your back."

"I'd expect nothing less." I laughed. "Actually, I just like to saunter. Also, I take pleasure in their displeasure. It's not a good trait."

She shrugged understanding and said, "Like one of your Dad's hound dogs, guarding a bleached bone nobody wants." I was touched by her remembering my father's hounds but perplexed by the analogy. Then, in a spot-on imitation of Mrs. Franz, she said, "Jake." I felt instantly chastened, so much so that I wanted to vow to walk fast in New York and other cities. Then I tried my imitation, adding a Franzian faux-query. "Kathy?"

"Not bad," Kathy said. "Amazing how she could say your name and let you know you'd been arrested, tried, convicted, and sentenced, all in the time it would take Whis to burp." She knocked back a shot of Jim Beam. "Dear Lord give me strength!" she said.

I laughed and lifted my glass of red wine. "To Mrs. Wiggins."

She and I weren't from Claytonville anymore, but neither were we not from Claytonville. Both of us might plausibly claim that we'd done well and been good, but who cares? For my part, I'd left the solar system in second grade and begun to get acquainted with the real world, but decades later I still tried to reconstruct the feeling that had sprung from a child's gazing at a poster in a classroom. In fact, I was gazing right then, looking through not at the scene at O'Hare when Kathy's words brought me back.

"She was something else, Jake. Vera."

"She sure was.... *Vera.*"

We hauled our baggage out of the bar and said goodbye.

Where Light Is a Place

Beverly Conner

Nineteen forty-eight. If you were young and understood your world from newsreels, it could seem as if everything important (like World War II) had already happened. How could you guess the Soviet Union would soon test its first A-bomb? Or McCarthy tell Truman the State Department was riddled with communists? True, W.H. Auden had signaled the era to come with his Pulitzer-prize winning *Age of Anxiety*, but poets, the newscaster chirped from the black and white movie screen, were seldom larky fellows. Even grownups sat in the dark, not imagining loyalty oaths or a swelling Hollywood blacklist. And Korea was still oceans away in most minds. So the present moment held people like the hesitation between breaths, the trough between waves. Like latency before adolescence, it was a time of treading water.

A month after eighth grade started at Las Olitas Elementary School, Palmer McNeil lay stomach-down, baking on the sultry autumn sand of Manhattan Beach, a white-sun town bordered by the emerald-green Pacific. On one side lay her eight-year-old sister Maggie and on the other the tanned blond boy who lately turned Palmer's pulse to flutterkicks – three California kids on three well-washed towels.

By summer's end, even Palmer with her freckles and fair skin had tanned to a ruddy glow, her dark hair, like Maggie's, sun-bleached at its tips. As the Saturday afternoon dozed past 3:30, other kids also trailing younger sisters or brothers headed for home, but Palmer wanted to stay as long as JJ was bedded down in the hot sand beside her.

For nearly a week, Maggie had been pestering Palmer to take her out into water over her head, and Palmer had put her off, for no particular reason beyond the fact that five years lay between them so she could. Besides, Maggie was still pretty young to take into deep water even if she was a sturdy dog-paddler.

Palmer felt the scatter of fine sand across her calves. Maggie was restless, and Palmer wanted to head off her sister's asking yet another time. And anyway JJ seemed ready to leave, his chin propped now on a forearm, one hand idly sifting sand, the mica glistening and blowing slightly as a late afternoon breeze came up.

Palmer rolled onto her side and lazily pushed herself up. Maggie was burying her sister's feet in a desultory way. "Well," Palmer asked her, "do you want to go in or not?" She jerked her head toward the surf and briskly brushed off her legs. "I guess this is as good a time as any."

All the little kids begged for this adventure because alone they were forbidden to venture past their waists, and not even that far if the undertow were strong. Maggie often dreamed of undertows, especially after a long day at the beach when her little brown body, sunburned and waterlogged, replayed at night the rhythms of waves pulling at her legs. She'd long known the difference between an everyday sort of undertow – the kind that was fun, trotting you back into the surf – and the bad ones on rough-water days when the beach slanted steep and dangerous, and your first step into the surf was already too deep.

Palmer noted the full tide with the surf running high, but the undertow still seemed mild. Teenage boys were bodysurfing. Few had the cash to buy the heavy, redwood surfboards they coveted, let alone a car to transport the six-foot boards between home and water, one end poking pridefully out a car window.

Some days the surf was rough enough to keep the little kids digging moats and building castles above the waterline. But as 13-year-olds, Palmer and her friends skipped only the darkest days when the ocean turned to slate and the waves rose high enough to spray fishermen on the long, tall Pier, waves that held their crest as they moved toward shore, then peaked before pounding into a back-breaking froth that could catch a swimmer and beat her into the sea-bottom. More than once, Palmer had her bathing cap ripped off her head. Girls joked about losing the tops of their swimsuits in a wild surf.

One boy had his neck broken in fifth grade when a wave carried him high into shore and dumped him headfirst into shallow water. He'd worn a neck brace the rest of the summer and half the school year. But by now, kids Palmer's age were good at gauging weather and surf, their instincts telling them what could be risked. It was a point of pride: only tourists got in trouble.

She stuffed her hair into her bathing cap, holding the white rubber away from each ear to make room, snapping the strap beneath her chin. Maggie's hair was a mop of saltwater tangles. Palmer had only started wearing a cap at the beach this year, along with her first two-piece suit that shimmered now in the sun like a pale peach shell.

Except it hadn't quite been her first, though she tried to forget the trouble over the original suit at the start of summer, one more brouhaha Daddy called it. Mother had taken Palmer to Jean's Apparel, and Palmer picked out a two-piece, navy blue Catalina in the newest latex fabric, really more than they could afford, but Mother said it was time for a grown-up bathing suit.

The first time Palmer wore the suit to the beach, she carefully rinsed it out afterwards and hung it on the line to dry. Before the sun set, the suit turned a mottled purple, like a bruise against the sky. Palmer actually cried. She couldn't wear such an ugly, faded thing; she'd rather go back to her old one-piece. In fact, the old suit did look better. Mother hugged her and promised they'd take care of it, but she had that nervous look on her face, as if her blue eyes had gone pale. Palmer wiped her tears away quickly.

Mother started drinking first thing the next morning, and by the time they walked into the store with the bathing suit, she was bristling with outrage.

"May I help you?" The saleswoman was about Mother's age, but very tan. She wore a navy skirt with a white blouse, a blue silk scarf knotted at her neck. Gold earrings dotted her ears. The woman's nails gleamed a dark red that matched her lipstick. Mother's lipstick, a pink shade, was crooked, and Palmer swallowed against the small panicked birds that darted in her stomach.

"I need to speak to the manager," Mother said, her feet planted slightly apart for balance, making her look ready for war.

The saleswoman's eyes narrowed. "I'm the only one here right now. What seems to be the problem?"

Mother was pulling the faded suit from a paper grocery bag. Palmer wished they'd kept the cream-colored bag that had Jean's Apparel printed in dark green letters. Half the suit fell onto the carpeted floor, and Palmer scooped it up. Mother snatched it away and thrust the suit at the woman. "Look at this!"

"Yes?"

"'Yes?' That's all you can say about shoddy merchandise that fades the first time it's worn?"

The saleswoman ran one blood-tipped nail over the fabric. "Our bathing suits are not guaranteed to be 100% colorfast. Naturally, the darker colors –"

"Well, why the hell didn't somebody mention that when we bought the damn thing?" Mother was leaning toward the woman who was trying to stand her ground.

"Did you dry it out of the sun?" she asked. "It should be hung in the shade for best –"

"In the shade? This is a bathing suit! My daughter wears it in and out of the water all day long – how is it going to dry out of the sun unless she strips it off and walks around naked? Or is that also what you recommend?"

Palmer touched her mother's forearm. That old, sweetish smell steamed off Claudia in the warm shop.

"Do you have your sales slip?" the saleswoman asked, raising her chin slightly.

Mother took a step toward the woman, who quickly began to examine the suit again. "We bought this two days ago. The suit fit fine and my daughter liked it. Why would we keep the receipt?" Mother shifted her pocketbook to her other arm and threw back her shoulders. "Naturally, we assume that Jean's stands behind its goddamn merchandise."

The saleswoman sighed. Heaven only knew what her boss was going to say. She looked at Palmer. "Would your daughter like to choose another suit in exchange?"

"Thank you," Mother said with dignity. She wobbled only slightly. Palmer's face felt stiff, even though they'd won – hadn't they?

Now Maggie scrambled up and raced for the water, sand flying behind her.

"Maybe I'll hang around for awhile," said JJ when Palmer stood up. She nodded at him before starting after Maggie who had already waded up to her knees. Together they splashed into the waves, then quickly ducked their shoulders under to put that first cold-water shock behind them. Palmer grabbed Maggie's hand.

It was fun jumping combers together, Palmer throwing her body side-first into each wave, one arm raised high to cut a swathe so that she took the surf's force, holding tight to Maggie's hand behind her. When the water deepened, Palmer struck out in a crawl with her sister hanging onto her shoulders. Before any time at all, they were safely beyond the breakers. Even with more white caps than

Palmer had noticed from shore, these dark green swells were a smooth payoff for battling through the surf.

Maggie was giggling, her hand hooked in one of Palmer's pale shoulder straps, her body streaming out behind as she kicked to help propel them along. A few years back, there'd been no one to take Palmer over her head when she was Maggie's age. Daddy was frank about his distaste for the beach. But Mother? Palmer didn't know why her mother seldom left the house except to walk that small radius down Manhattan Avenue, doing errands at the post office and drugstore, at the market and finally the dime store before turning back towards home. Little more than a six-block journey, round-trip. Even her AA meetings were only a few blocks away at the Community Church.

So with friends or by herself, Palmer had inched her way into deep water, first in swimming pools where she'd learned to swim with Girl Scout lessons, then in the ocean where she practiced jumping waves and ducking her head under them.

Today Palmer was glad the waves were not so big. It could be hard to hold onto Maggie if a wave gave them a good tumble. Before long, her sister would learn the waves, first bobbing under smaller ones and opening her eyes to look upward into the green-white bubbles, that swirl of diamonds as a wave churned overhead, to feel its pull and power so that in the calm she would know the wave had passed and it would be safe to come up.

Some kids held their noses when they ducked under, but Palmer would teach Maggie to close her nasal passages far back, like a mouth breather, to hold her breath as long as she needed and then blow out like a young whale as she surfaced. You learned to crouch or lie on your stomach, hands and forearms gripping the bottom sand that was swept smooth of shell in these southern waters. Most of the time Palmer just dove deeply, her belly skimming bottom, to let the wave roll on over her. Even so, now and then a pounder reached down to churn up sand and swimmer alike.

"See how I'm treading water now? It's just like dog paddling except you stay straight up and down and don't go anywhere. Work your legs like a bicycle."

Maggie gulped a shot of salt water and coughed. "Let me just dog paddle."

"Okay, but go around me in a circle so you stay close."

And like a little dolphin, her wet head jerking with the rhythm of arms and legs, Maggie paddled fiercely in water many times deeper than she was tall. Her eyes were wide with the enormity of the sea. Palmer never took her own eyes off her sister, feeling the responsibility of where they'd traveled grow heavier. Except for the scream of a tern high above them, there was no sound out here except the ceaseless wind and water.

And Palmer suddenly saw how her parents might view this ocean adventure. She glanced toward shore, and her stomach lurched. How could they have drifted this far out without her even noticing? People on the beach looked tiny, and some of them seemed to be waving. One figure detached itself, and Palmer thought she saw the kelly green of JJ's swim trunks.

She looked back at Maggie. The water around them was roiled in an odd way, different from the usual chop. Another white cap smacked Maggie in the face, throwing off the rhythm of her dog paddle. Palmer was beside her in two strokes.

"Grab onto my shoulders," she said. "It's time to go back." Palmer strained to make her voice sound calm, but the truth was she'd finally snapped to their situation. How long, she wondered, had they been in this riptide? She was furious she hadn't spotted the river of foam that was right now sweeping them out to sea.

She peered back at the beach, hoping the lifeguard wasn't swimming toward them that very moment, his buoy streaming behind him. It would be humiliating, and besides, she was sure they could make it in on their own. Didn't the guards have to call your folks when they made a rescue? Mother would lay down a beach-ban on both of them, for sure.

"Why aren't we swimming in?" Maggie yelled.

"We're in a rip." Palmer made her voice calm. "But I know what to do. Just don't let go!"

She felt her sister's fingers bite into her shoulders, but Maggie didn't make another sound. Palmer put all her energy into her crawl, breathing with every other arm pull. She was moving them parallel to the shore, as if swimming across a river. She could see why swimmers panicked at finding themselves so far out to sea. The ocean looked vast from here, and Palmer had a prickly sense of creature-filled depths beneath their white, kicking limbs. She'd often thought Maggie's little seal-head was cute, but now she imagined the view from below – the two of them on the surface of the water, how they genuinely looked like seals, and seals were sharkfood.

Stay calm, she told herself, stay calm. Great Whites

were so rare in these waters that the newspaper printed every shark attack, and there weren't many. Everyone knew the real danger, especially to tourists, was fatigue or cramps from trying to swim straight to shore against the riptide that was sweeping them toward the horizon.

Once she and Maggie could swim across and out of the rip, the swells would push them toward shore; the trick was to stay afloat. If she didn't get too tired and could keep swimming, all the better. Even so, Palmer felt the growing temptation to turn directly toward shore, like the pull of a magnet she knew she had to resist.

But in that next moment, the texture of the water turned silky. She looked back at the riffled channel that was so hard to spot if you were already in it, and wondered about the chances of a rip's widening, a net to capture them once more. Like a wave breaking over her head, she realized for the first time that gaps in ocean lore could cost lives.

Still she resisted the siren's lure of the shore and kept swimming parallel to the beach. Her arms felt heavy, but when she looked behind her again, the rip seemed far away. Safely out of the treacherous current, they now merely had the swim into shore to worry about! While they'd been swimming out of the riptide, they'd been swept even farther from the safety of the beach. Palmer longed to feel sand beneath her feet right now.

Glancing toward the Pier, she could see they were beyond the end of it, and she shivered slightly. She'd never been out this deep alone, though lots of times, she and JJ and other kids had swum as a group as far out as the Roundhouse perched nearly at the Pier's end, then turned and ridden the swells in. She was sure she could manage it alone, but she'd never before had her little sister hanging onto her back.

"We're outta th' rip, Mags – headed in now."

"Okay," her sister said, teeth chattering from cold or fright or both.

Palmer knew she had to take it easy, not muscle her way through the swim. She used the slight momentum of the swells. Any other time she was so buoyant in the salt water she could tread water just by using her legs, her hands raised high above the surface – a showoff trick. But now Maggie's body hung like a bedraggled anchor behind her.

On the beach more people seemed to be gathering and waving, and she thought she saw the red-suited lifeguard wading out into the shallow water. Adrenaline surged into her stroke. She kept checking her distance by looking across the water at the Pier. They were making progress, opposite the bait house now.

The swim out had been easy and lighthearted, but now Palmer was breathing hard. Her legs felt cold while her arms burned. The strap of her bathing cap cut into her neck. But they were inching toward the line of breakers, and at last she felt the first strong swell lift and push them forward, then another, until Palmer heard the first wave break behind them and suddenly they were in the midst of them. She caught Maggie's hand and yelled, "Hold your breath!" The wave tumbled them forward where another swell rose up, blinding them for a second to everything except high green water. They slipped over the top before it broke. Another wave rolled them into its crest and when they slid down the other side, Palmer was grateful as hard sand brushed her toes.

Suddenly a man rose up in front of them, shaking the water from his hair. They were face-to-face with the lifeguard, and he didn't look happy.

"Didn't you kids see that rip?" he yelled. "You had no business out that far!" The guard's face was red, and he made no move to help Palmer pull Maggie the last yards to where they could walk through the waves. Instead, he reeled in the torpedo buoy that streamed behind his chest harness.

"Sorry," Palmer said. She was shaking now. Cold, relief, embarrassment – one feeling after another smacked her in the face like the white caps only minutes before. Why did it have to be the redheaded guard, the one they called Terry? He was even cuter up close. Ever since fifth grade, Palmer had had a crush on him, always checking the lifeguard tower to see if he were the one on duty.

He scowled at her, his eyebrows one furious line above his green eyes. "You knew you were in a rip out there?"

Palmer nodded. People around them laughed and began to walk away. They'd lined up to see a rescue that had petered out. Only the little kids were hanging around to watch the lifeguard bawl these two out. The guard secured the buoy line and tucked it under his arm. He looked at Maggie who was shivering like a little rat, then back at Palmer. His face softened to a mere frown.

"I've seen you around here, kid." It sounded to her like a warning. "You swim okay, otherwise I'd a been out there," he gestured toward the horizon. Freckles fine as sand sprayed across his face and shoulders. "And then it would have been an official rescue." He didn't smile.

"Don't swim out that far," he ordered Palmer, "and don't ever take her out there again."

He turned to Maggie whose thin arms crossed her chest, clutching her elbows. "Don't go in over your head until you can swim the distance. Got that?" She nodded miserably. "Keep your feet on the bottom," he added, as if she still didn't understand. She nodded again. He shifted his stare to Palmer, then turned abruptly and marched out of the water toward the lifeguard tower.

For a second Palmer was too mortified to move. The kids around them giggled until she shot them a dark look. She unsnapped her cap and pulled it off. "C'mon, let's get warm."

Someone splashed up behind them. "You okay?" JJ stood knee-deep in the water. He'd heard every embarrassing word.

"Oh, yeah," she said, rolling her eyes at him. She took a deep breath and rubbed her arms, trying to relax so she'd stop shaking. "It was dumb, but I knew we were okay."

"Sure. I was watching, too. Almost swam out myself," he added.

"Thanks, but we were okay."

"Sure," he said, walking beside them, up and across the beach.

When they reached their towels, Maggie dropped like a ragdoll and burrowed directly into the hot sand. "Sorry," she mumbled, not even sure what for.

Palmer toweled off quickly, spread the towel and lay beside her. JJ threw himself down next to Palmer. "It wasn't your fault," she said to Maggie. "Just don't tell Mother, or we'll never see the beach again as long as we live, and I'm not kidding!"

Maggie nodded and wriggled deeper, her cheek against the sand. Palmer turned her head toward JJ. He reached over and squeezed her hand, his palm hot around her chilled fingers. The sun beat down on them, and Palmer closed her eyes, trying to still her trembling and shutting out the waves behind her and the deep currents in her head that still held Great White shadows swimming like bad dreams. The onshore breeze whispered across her outstretched legs.

Gradually, the screen behind her eyelids (where this drama of her own making still played out) darkened softly to violet, the way she liked to imagine the deepest parts of the ocean. Today, so far out in the water, nothing had seemed soft, but now with her hand curled warm in JJ's, her breathing slowed and her body drifted on sun-spotted swells of approaching sleep.

In January the gods of strange weather surprised Southern California with a 1949 storm for the record books. Sometime during the night, against all climatic odds, it began to snow. Mother and Daddy awakened Palmer sleeping in the top bunk, Maggie below her.

"Look outside," Daddy whispered. "You won't believe what you see." He slid open the peeling, wood frame of the window just a foot from their beds in the cramped sunroom where the girls slept in the tiny beach house.

The Shack they had christened it, knowing they were lucky to rent any place at all. After nine months in Portland, they had moved back from Oregon once the war ended. For "opportunity's sake," Daddy said. Because he lost his job, said Mother.

Now, just outside their bedroom window, snow swirled through the blackness as far as they could see, and all the while just a block and a half away, the constant rush of the surf sounded through the night air.

Palmer struggled to slide out of her bunk onto the cold linoleum floor. "What time is it?"

"About four in the morning," Daddy said, smiling up into the dark sky. Mother stood behind him, watching over his shoulder.

Maggie crawled from bed to put her arm out the window. She turned her palm up to catch the flakes and brought them like frosted lace to her tongue. Palmer stood transfixed beside her. The salt air smelled sweetly icy.

"I'll put on some coffee," Mother said, backing away from the open window.

Neither of the girls had ever seen snow. And though the parents had fled Midwest storms years before, even they seemed stunned. The coastal snowfall that year – snow that for one night and day drifted over the beaches as if millions of seagulls had shed frozen feathers – was a California miracle.

Half an hour later, bundled into layers of clothing, they were driving through the still-dark morning to the hills of Palos Verdes to play in snowdrifts. The steam from Mother's coffee mug dimmed the inside of the windshield, and Daddy wiped at it with his bare hand, snorting impatiently and glancing pointedly at Mother's cup. Palmer could feel old ghosts rise up in the darkened car.

Before they left the house, each wearing two pairs of socks, their feet in rubber galoshes, the girls drank hot, sweetened coffee-milk, dunking buttered toast into their mugs.

Mother had poured herself a second cup while Daddy warmed up the Plymouth. She disappeared into their bedroom, pulling the floral curtain behind her. Only the bathroom and the house's front door, which both opened right into the kitchen, boasted real doors. Like many of the cottages hastily built near the beach, it was no more than a small kitchen and living room, a bedroom alcove, and a bath. The narrow sun porch that served as the girls' bedroom was the only room that faced the ocean, but the new apartment house next door – only feet away, really – blocked any view and most of the light, so that by two in the afternoon the house was dim even on the brightest summer day.

Palmer heard her mother's dresser drawer slide open. A half-minute passed, the drawer slid shut, and then Mother appeared through the curtain, her face already softened, the mug in her hand.

"C'mon, Sleepyheads, stop gathering wool. Your father's waiting!"

And now as Daddy drove slowly toward Palos Verdes, familiar landmarks turned wondrous, draped in strange, snowy shawls. He drove past the sandstone public library, past the shoe repair shop, the Rexall drugstore, all the while muttering under his breath – Jesus H. Christ! – and shifting gears roughly. Mother gazed serenely out of the windshield, but the set of her shoulders had squared, as if braced for battle.

"Don't spoil this, Daniel." She drained her mug and set it carefully by her feet.

"It's not me who needs the warning."

Palmer leaned over the front seat between them. The cadence in her father's voice signaled danger. It felt to her as if the air in the car were being swallowed up, and she took a deep breath. "Are we almost there? How far now, Daddy?"

"You getting wheezy, princess?" He glanced at Mother, blame smoldering in his eyes.

"Of course she's not! Or if she is, it's because you dragged her out of bed in this freezing –"

"Judas Priest, Claudia, here we go –"

"No," Palmer said, sweating now in her jacket and two sweaters. An asthma attack would turn them home. "I'm okay. Honest. Why don't we just stop here and play in the snow? This looks like a good place!"

"Here," echoed Maggie, "and I have to go to the bathroom, too."

Daddy glanced in his rearview mirror at his younger daughter, gauging her need. "In a minute, Magpie. Let's see if somebody has opened early." He swiped again at the windshield. "Okay, up there ahead."

He made a left turn into the Texaco station, and Maggie was out the door almost before he stopped. "Whoa, kiddo. Palmer, you go with your sister."

"But I don't need to!" Palmer's voice was a nervous whine. She didn't want to leave them alone together just now.

"I said –"

"Oh, for heaven's sake, I'll go!" But Mother had trouble opening the passenger-side door. Daddy didn't reach across to help her. Finally she shoved it hard with her shoulder. The momentum nearly toppled her out of the car, but she straightened, swung her slender legs to the side and stood up shakily.

"It sure doesn't take much anymore," Daddy said.

Mother ignored him and followed Maggie to the restroom, her head high with wounded dignity. She called over her shoulder, "You want cigarettes?" but Daddy shook his head. She pressed her hand protectively against the bulge in her pocket. Palmer imagined she could hear the half-pint gurgle.

Daddy leaned back against the seat, and Palmer reached over to touch his shoulder, but he didn't move. Now the car seemed cold, even though Daddy kept the engine running, and Palmer could see her breath like a warning spirit that had been there as far back as she could remember.

When they were all in the car again, Daddy drove in silence. Finally he whispered, "You've had yourself quite a snootful!" But the fight had gone out of Mother, and she slumped in the front seat, head thrown back, her hair a dark halo. Soon her mouth fell open, and she began to snore lightly.

Still, they did play in their first-ever-snow until the girls' toes began to burn with cold. The snow-covered fields of Palos Verdes gleamed above the ocean, smooth as a ghostly airstrip, and below them green phosphorescence flickered in the waves that swept toward the cliffs. Daddy stood near the edge, looking through the falling snow at the surf below until Palmer and Maggie tugged at him to come play.

Mother slept through their snowball fights, their

whoops and snow angels and miniature snowmen, slept all the way home in the car where Daddy threatened to leave her all night even if she did freeze her ass off – pardon me, girls – but he finally shook her roughly and then half carried, half dragged her inside, through the kitchen and the curtained doorway of their bedroom where Palmer saw him throw her down on the bed. Palmer followed behind and began to take off her mother's shoes.

"I'll take care of it, princess," Daddy said and sent them off to their bunks in the pale early morning light. They were both so cold that Palmer crawled in next to Maggie's sturdy little body, and they pressed their feet against one another's legs, squealing, until Daddy yelled for them to pipe down.

At last they warmed up and settled in for a few more hours of sleep. Everyone overslept and Daddy left for work late without breakfast. Mother was cross and sat in her chenille robe over coffee at the kitchen table, smoking one cigarette after another. The girls stayed home from school but were glad to escape the house. Dressed warmly, they ran down to the beach to play in the snow that still carpeted the sand.

Sometime before lunch, the sun broke through the high overcast, misty at first, then brighter and brighter. And for just a few moments before the few inches of snow melted into the sand, the beach gleamed, sun-struck and blinding, a silver-white ribbon that trimmed the blue Pacific as far north and south as they could see. Like that albino snake kept at school, Palmer told her mother, when it slipped out of its old skin and looked so clean and new.

During the school year, it seemed to Palmer that so much of life happened in the afternoons. After school there was the dash home to change clothes and grab a snack before biking or roller skating on The Strand, saving homework for after dinner. Eighth grade wasn't turning out to be all that hard. And on weekends year-round, double features at the La Mar filled both Saturday and Sunday afternoons with suspense: men came home from the war with mechanical hooks where hands should have been; cattlemen fought range wars with sheepherders over grazing rights; spunky Jeanne Crain helped her G.I. husband turn from soldier to college student; and Olivia de Haviland fought for her sanity in *The Snake Pit*.

Drama could lurk at home, as well as at the movies. If Mother started drinking in the morning, then by mid-afternoon she might be passed out on the couch, lost to herself and to them as well. Palmer tried to predict these times that flew at her like scavenging gulls, but since Claudia herself didn't seem to know what set off a drinking bout, there wasn't much hope for anyone else to guess right. Mostly Palmer tried not to let her thoughts wander home. Mother kept slipping back into drinking – especially once Daddy began traveling with his new job.

But on this windswept Monday when Palmer dashed in from school, Mother was humming in the steamy kitchen making homemade noodles. Palmer could smell the soup stock before she even opened the door. On the back of the stove, the Easter turkey carcass simmered gently, along with carrots and celery, onions, cloves, and bay leaves. Mother turned to kiss Palmer. A broom lay across the backs of two kitchen chairs, its handle draped with clean tea-towels. One by one, Mother hung homemade noodles to dry from this carefully balanced rack.

The onshore winds had been blowing hard over Easter vacation when there'd been an actual sandstorm, keeping everyone indoors. Each day had been cold and sunny with the wind screaming around the beach houses. Silt piled up inside on windowsills, even when windows were kept locked. Sand blew into people's hair, crunched between their teeth, and irritated eyes already red from the previous day's blow. Housewives went crazy, trying to keep floors swept up. They covered food and even swiped at clean dishes when the table was set. Children were scolded for not putting lids back on butter dishes or sugar bowls.

Every afternoon Claudia gave the girls damp rags to dust with, the cloths making dark swaths across the furniture. Maggie whined at night when Claudia cleaned her ears of grit, and Daniel complained the sand was going to blast the paint right off his car. With the sun in a cloud-scoured sky, its light was diffused by blowing sand, like a movie star's close-up shot through layers of gauze.

Secretly, Palmer enjoyed the storm. It had somehow shuttered the house in a cozy way. And besides, she didn't care if her parents grumbled good-naturedly about winds that howled in from the ocean and over the beach, scooping up sand to hurl at the town.

It was the edginess in those other winds that sent Palmer scurrying home after school to check on Claudia.

Santanas, her father called them, using the old Spanish term. Devil winds. But the newscasters called them Santa Ana's ww powerful winds out of the east that swept down from the mountains, skimming arid deserts, to arrive hot and dry, frazzling nerves and fraying tempers. Winds that always seemed to find a spark somewhere, usually from a cigarette thrown out of a car or a campfire carelessly smothered, to fan into firestorms that destroyed acres of forest and chaparral, and sometimes homes. Coyotes, cougars, jackrabbits – all fled the infernos. Nests and young were consumed. Maggie hugged her cat close when the radio reported wildlife lost.

Claudia hated the devil winds. Daniel said it had to do with ions in the air. Claudia said she didn't care what it had to do with, they made her jumpy as hell. And all too often, when the Santa Ana's began to blow, Claudia started in to drink.

Then Palmer would scurry home, sometimes running downhill the last quarter mile from school with those devil winds howling at her back, to find Mother passed out on the living room couch. Palmer would wash up the breakfast dishes sitting crusty in the sink and sweep out the kitchen. It wasn't that she cared anything about housekeeping, but she hoped that by making the house look normal her father would overlook her mother's drinking, and Palmer could hold their arguments at bay for another night.

She'd scrub potatoes and put them in the oven to bake, though Claudia would only make a pretense of eating if she even came to dinner. Usually before Palmer finished these chores, her mother would rouse herself from the couch to walk with extraordinary care into the kitchen. "When your father gets home," she'd say with that odd dignity of the drinker, "inform him I'm unwell." She'd make for her bed, passing Palmer and trailing a scent of persimmons set too long to ripen on top of the icebox.

But today was a safe day, a Monday to be snug inside. With Mother busy cooking and the buttery scent of noodle soup filling the house, maybe her mother would even forget about the dusting for one afternoon. Palmer headed for her father's easy chair – the one in which he read each evening's *Herald-Express*.

Most nights before bed, he still read aloud to Palmer and Maggie. They perched on the broad arms of that chair, leaning into his warm shoulders. But sometimes he shook them off. "C'mon, girls, give your ol' man some breathing room!"

They'd straighten up and he'd go back to fiddling with the wooden match he always picked up in the kitchen before reading aloud, sliding his thumb and index finger up and down in the steady rhythm that Palmer found comforting. The one time she tried it, she ran a splinter into her thumb.

Claudia said he picked books too adult for the girls, especially for Maggie, like *Treasure Island* and *Huckleberry Finn*, but he said if he didn't enjoy the book himself, he'd just nod off. Besides, he wasn't so sure the books were too old for smart kids. Lately he was reading them *Tom Sawyer*. The girls liked Tom even better than Huck.

Before kids turned twelve, they were restricted to the children's section of the Manhattan Beach Library. So in years past, like a cartoon character scooting from tree to rock to bush, Palmer had practiced sneaking into the adult stacks. Furtively, she devoured the lean cowboys and sassy women of Zane Grey. She read all of Sinclair Lewis, and pored with special attention over an illustrated anatomy text.

She learned to digest whole portions of books before a librarian could swoop down and march her back to the children's section. Once she realized that escaping detection lay primarily in keeping still, she managed to start and finish *The Red Pony* all in one afternoon behind a pillar. She also learned that people in charge weren't right about everything and she didn't always have to obey. Mostly she came to trust her imagination to ease her through the pangs of daily reality.

For their part, Claudia and Daniel seemed neither impressed nor unimpressed with her reading. It was something they all did, including Maggie who was racing through Albert Payson Terhune and slept with *Misty of Chincoteague* under her pillow. Library books formed the bulk of their entertainment, along with radio and the girls' matinees.

Friday nights after dinner Daniel made his special popcorn – butter, salt, and a dash of sugar. On Saturday mornings, she and Maggie loved the butter-soggy popcorn more than Wheaties, and they'd polish off the leftovers while listening to their favorite radio program, *Let's Pretend*. One thing about fairy tales – books or broadcast – no matter how many witches, ogres, giants, or trolls loomed in dark forests, every Saturday morning the prince married the princess. And in the end, children were always safe.

Mouths stuffed with popcorn, they sang along softly with the commercial that opened the show where even the ads were upbeat and wholesome: Cream of Wheat is so good to eat that we eat it every day!

They listened to *Lux Radio Theater* and thrilled to the dramas of *Grand Central Station*. Once Daddy caught the opening and pronounced it all a bit overwrought. Palmer wondered if he resented "the glitter and swank of Park Avenue." For her part, these imagined lives on the radio, in books and in movies, buoyed her spirit. It was the undertows of everyday life that knocked your feet out from under you.

So on this first Monday after Easter vacation, Palmer read for over an hour before Mother called her to set the table and slice a cantaloupe for dinner. When Daniel breezed in from work, his cheeks ruddy from the wind, Mother had biscuits baking to go with the turkey soup. Maggie was playing with paper dolls at the kitchen table.

"Mmm, smells good in here," he said, kissing each one. "Let me just write up my paper work – move over there, Magpie – then we can dive in."

"Everything's all ready," Claudia said mildly, taking the biscuits out of the oven.

"Can't relax until I'm done, not with leaving tomorrow."

"Leaving?"

Daniel smacked himself in the forehead. "I didn't mention it? Smitty's sending me up to Santa Barbara for the rest of the week. Back Friday, as usual."

"But I've made enough soup for an army –"

He swung his sample case onto a chair. "I just found out myself the other day."

"If you'd told me, I wouldn't have gone to all this work." She slid the biscuits onto a plate.

"Look, I'm sorry, but sometimes until I actually have to pack, even I don't remember my schedule." He studied her face. "C'mon, Claudia, just be glad I'm working. You and the girls will gobble this soup up."

Palmer figured they'd eat it every night all week long, which was okay with her. She loved her mother's soup. But Mother didn't look happy.

"I *am* glad you're working," she said quietly.

Daddy looked at her sharply, but Mother had turned to the stove and was stirring the soup.

This time Palmer guessed right, though she couldn't see what practical good it did any of them. Daddy left early the next morning, and by the time school let out on Tuesday, Mother was as bad as Palmer had ever seen her. Wednesday and Thursday, too. The girls ate soup every night, the two of them quiet at the kitchen table, Mother passed out on the other side of the bedroom curtain. They listened to their radio programs and read library books. Palmer did her homework while Maggie colored, and they put themselves to bed. Nothing they hadn't done before.

The wind blew all week, the April sun thin and pitiless. Late Friday afternoon Palmer crept into the house. She'd stayed at her friend Bonnie's after school for as long as she could. Maggie was probably still playing with toy horses at her girlfriend Nancy's house.

But Claudia was up, sober and alert. She called out from her bedroom, "I'm straightening up in here, Palmer, so you get the dusting done. Your father will be home tonight, and I'm going to fix spaghetti. Don't plan on reading away the whole afternoon." She sounded on edge – not unusual when she quit drinking abruptly. "Set the hamburger out."

Almost giddy with relief, Palmer opened the ice box and pulled out the butcher paper bundle of ground beef. By now, even she was tired of turkey soup. But more wonderful than spaghetti, Daddy would be home soon, and Mother had already stopped drinking – probably on a dime that morning, sobering up fast, the way she sometimes did. Maybe Palmer wouldn't have to pay so much attention for awhile.

The strain of the past few days began to leak out of Palmer's bones; she felt relaxed and even a little sleepy, as if she'd spent the afternoon swimming against a winter surf.

Sobering up after a three-day binge, and a bad one at that, Mother would naturally be irritable. It was an old pattern: hard drinking for a few days, especially when Daddy took to the road for a sales trip. Then the abrupt stop – going on the wagon, they called it – a tense time for everybody but far better than the drinking. With their father's new job and Mother's lapses, the girls sometimes felt as if both parents had set off on separate journeys away from home.

Palmer overhead the term drying-out from her father and his friend Lars as the men finished fishing from the Pier one Saturday afternoon. They'd been talking about Claudia before they saw Palmer waiting there with her bike. She understood what they meant. Sobering up, her mother would take a hard look around the house and see how things had gotten out of hand while she'd been sleeping it off. If Daniel were out of town, dishes would be piled on the drain boards, clothes thrown over furniture, and Maggie's toys strewn around the living room. With her father gone, Palmer herself had no interest in making things look normal.

One time when Daniel was on the road and Claudia was drinking, the girls ran out of food. Because Palmer always knew where her mother hid her pocketbook, it wasn't a real emergency. She was used to helping herself to grocery money. This time, feeling lazy and knowing better, she walked down to the market and bought two Cokes and a large bag of potato chips. Maggie was tickled with their dinner. During the night, the unrinsed Coke bottle and a few stray chips attracted the tiny brown grease ants that everyone at the beach guarded against. They wove a path like a ribbon from the trash container, up the front of the silverware drawer, and onto the drain board. In the morning a sobered-up Claudia bawled Palmer out good for that one, though Palmer wasn't sure if her mother were more angry about the ants or the pop-and-chips dinner.

When her mother came back (that was how Palmer thought of it), it could be one more time to be on guard. Don't bother Mother, she's nervous today was how Claudia herself put it, smoking steadily, her hands shaky, the tips of her first two fingers stained amber as the camel on the front of the cigarette package.

But today, knowing her father was due home and lulled by Mother's brisk voice, Palmer missed signs that she was normally good at reading. Certain other afternoons when she walked in the door, the very air — too still in some way — told her all she needed to know, the clues obvious from the breakfast clutter or knickknacks tipped over as her mother wandered the small rooms, drinking through the day's long, muted sunlight.

From a bowl on the drainboard, Palmer grabbed a tart green apple. Even its color said go right ahead, take a big bite, we're not the dangerous red of Snow White's poisonous fruit. She would change her clothes, take care of the dusting, and maybe there'd still be time to read. She was only a chapter away from the end of that early California story where a love like Ramona's would suffer from a changing world she couldn't control.

A crash from the bedroom startled her, like a perfume bottle flung against the wall. Before Palmer could even move, Mother burst through the curtains, her face white as apple's flesh, eyes stretched in terror, screaming at Palmer to get down on the floor right now! For a second Palmer was disoriented, like riding in a car when sunlit buildings flashed by. The apple tumbled out of her hand.

At the same moment, Maggie banged into the house.

"Get down!" Claudia screamed. "Stay away from the window! Those curtains are open!" Mother half-tackled Maggie, the two of them falling onto the kitchen floor. Claudia pulled Maggie across the linoleum toward the table.

"What's wrong?" Maggie cried.

"Under the table – now!" Claudia whispered frantically, scrabbling on her knees, clutching at Maggie. She flung the kitchen chairs out of her way, one toppling backwards. "Get under here!" Her teeth were gritted. "They'll see you!" She made a grab for Palmer's skirt as she shoved Maggie ahead of her under the table. Palmer squatted down; Maggie whimpered.

"Who are you talking about?" Palmer tried to sound calm, but her heart banged away in her chest.

Panting, Claudia reached out and caught her by a handful of hair. Palmer lost her balance and fell; the three of them knotted together under the table. She gasped with pain.

"Shhh!" Claudia spit at them. "Don't you think they can hear you? It's a wonder they let Maggie in the house!"

Palmer pried her mother's fingers out of her hair and rubbed her scalp. "Mother, who – ?"

"Those men out there!"

Maggie started to wail, and Claudia clapped her hand over her daughter's mouth.

"Where?" Palmer whispered, tremors now in her own chest.

Anger edged the panic in Claudia's voice. "For god's sake, they're standing right across the alley." She pointed. "By the telephone pole!"

Even from under the table, Palmer could peer outside over the window's low sill. No one stood by the telephone pole.

Trying to shelter both girls with her body, Claudia was keening, "Stay down, stay down, stay down!"

But Palmer raised her head again to look past her mother. She could see the empty alley, but someone must be out there. Men who were menacing the three of them as they crouched helpless inside the flimsy house with its one and only door unlocked. Then like a Saturday cartoon, the sudden image of the Three Little Pigs cornered by the Big Bad Wolf ballooned in her mind, and Palmer let out an hysterical giggle.

Just that fast, her mother's hand snaked out and slapped her hard across the back of the head. Her mother who never even spanked them hit Palmer hard enough to knock her over, hands flailing to keep her balance, catching the hem of the kitchen curtain and pulling it all – curtain and rod – clattering onto the floor, revealing the street empty from end to terrifying end.

"See?" said her mother. "Right there!"

Bent over Maggie – who was staring out at the empty alley, her tears stifled by astonishment – Claudia cradled her baby-daughter. Palmer turned back to them. She understood the terrible truth now. Pity strong as an undertow washed over her, and she wrapped her arms around them both, trying to shush her mother, to comfort her bewildered sister, rocking them all back and forth in some tidal rhythm, herself crying now, silent tears for her beloved mother who had clearly gone insane.

And that was where Daniel found them, in the near-dark, after he'd parked the car and lugged his sample case into the house, switching on the overhead light. Maggie had wet her pants. The little kitchen, closed up tight against the endlessly blowing sand, was humid with pee and tears, wheezing and terror.

Claudia was still babbling, wondering how Daniel had made it in to rescue them. He tried to take hold of her, but she was too frightened of dark strangers to be comforted. The curtains and rod were twisted around each other on the floor. On the drain board, watery blood dripped from the package of warm hamburger.

Daniel forced her to swallow four Empirin tablets with a glass of water, and he sent Palmer and Maggie off to take a hot bath. Through the closed door, they could hear him murmuring to Claudia in the kitchen. Their voices rose and fell and then moved to the bedroom, her mother occasionally shrill, her father more and more exasperated.

The sudden silence was both a relief and a worry. From opposite ends of the bath tub, Palmer and Maggie looked at each other over their comic books. Finally Palmer said, "Turn on more hot," and Maggie wriggled to the middle to get out of the way of the steaming rush from the old, pitted faucet.

When the girls finally emerged, pink and sweet smelling in their pajamas, the hot water exhausted, Claudia seemed to be asleep. On one side of her face a shadow darkened a swollen cheek. Her father was talking to Lars on the telephone.

"My god," he said, "DT's! Can you believe it?" Palmer listened closely. "Late afternoon, near as I can figure. Look, I gotta go; the girls are out of the tub. I have to tell them something."

But as Palmer heated up the very last of the turkey soup, all three seemed to be listening hard to the silence from the other side of the curtain. Maggie, who usually saved her noodles for the end, left half her soup uneaten. Daddy tossed out the spoiled meat and wiped up the mess. He rinsed out their three bowls. Like the three bears, Palmer thought, with Goldilocks asleep in one bed.

"Leave these," he said, though washing up was her job. "And the pan, too."

Maggie's eyes looked dull as old agates. Daddy dried his hands, then hugged and kissed them. "Your mother is sure to be better tomorrow. Go on to bed now."

In the sunroom, Palmer crawled after Maggie into the narrow bottom bunk. She held Maggie who held onto her cat, the three of them spoon-style. Despite the hot bath, Maggie was trembling. Palmer remembered how cold they'd been the day they were caught in the riptide and the night they played in the snowstorm. How even faced with that frozen miracle, Mother had been apart from them, Daddy standing on the high cliff, watching snow fall into the ocean below.

Now sleep seemed anchored out-of-reach in the dark. For a long time they lay quiet and listened to the sound of sand caught up in the wind's harsh breath.

The Bear

Ann Putnam

The bear is *dead*, I told the kids, so there isn't anything to worry about anymore. They told us at the park entrance that the bear is dead. They said they are sure they shot the bear who killed the boy and girl sleeping in their tent down by the lake. Still, we have seen signs everywhere warning of grizzly bears, though I imagine it's just to be on the safe side. Yesterday, for example, they closed the trail to Iceberg Ridge because some hikers had seen a bear just off the trail, so it just shows how cautious everybody has become.

It is early August and bears are moving down to feed on the berries on the slopes. But the bear attack by the lake, so close to the campgrounds, was a completely freakish thing, they have assured us. The action of a deranged bear. But as a precaution they have told us to stay on the trails, to make lots of noise, and to watch carefully for signs of bears. Like what, I wonder? Bear droppings? How would we recognize those? A dog's droppings look like Lincoln Logs. These would be huge, dark steaming mounds, I imagine. They give us a list of things believed to attract bears. It's a strange list: food, of course, but perfume, and insect repellent, and menstrual blood, and sex? Though the newspapers, which have described every bloody detail, said there was no food near the tent that night, that the girl was not having her period, that the boy and girl had not been making love. They were just asleep in their tent on the beach near the lake.

We have come here for our vacation. Last year our little boy was sick for most of the year, and so we all needed a vacation, and since all that is behind us now, this is supposed to be a sort of celebration as well as a holiday. But we didn't know anything about the bear maulings until yesterday at the park entrance. We've come here to see the mountains and the lake and to hike on the trails to the alpine meadows. My husband and my children have never been here before, but I came here with my parents and my grandfather when I was ten years old. We lived in the east then and my grandfather, who lived in the west, came to meet us here. We are in Glacier National Park, in Montana, at a place called Swift Current, which lies in a valley surrounded on all sides by mountains. But there are trails you can take that go so high you can look across the valley right at the tops of the mountains. From there the piece of sky you see from below widens as far as you can look. To climb this high and see out over the valley is one of the things we want to do.

I haven't been here since I was ten and I am stunned that it seems just the same. No Holiday Inn or Jack in the Box or McDonald's. Still just the one long building which holds the little restaurant, a small grocery, and a gift shop. This, and the cabins, the lavatory, and the tent sites which are now closed to overnight campers. They do not want anyone sleeping in tents in this valley.

Yesterday I went off by myself and took the path across the courtyard, past the bathrooms, and down toward the gift shop, pretending I was ten years old and had just come here from the east to meet my grandfather. I looked at the path and my feet walking it, watching my tennis shoes and white socks and my ankles, and pretended I was ten. It was secret and fun. I remembered how to take the path to the gift shop where I had spent hours looking at the rocks and Indian beads and rings. I opened the door and there was my little boy standing by the rows of agates, rubbing one between his fingers. I stepped back and watched him from the door, though he never saw me. And then I walked back to the cabin. Later I sat on the cabin steps and looked at the mountain in front of us. It is the highest mountain in the valley and I remembered how the sun would reach it first in the morning and go down behind it at night. The bands of rocks running orange and horizontal across the mountain made me think of Indians and the west and my tall, strong grandfather.

We've come here to see the mountains and the alpine meadows and the lake, which is the lowest point in the valley. The lake trail is the only one that takes you down. From there you have to tilt your head back to see the tops of the mountains. I can remember how my grandfather and I would walk to the lake in the evening to fish.

I remember his large hands like paws and his flat thumbs threading the salmon eggs onto the hook for me.

He could thread them onto the hooks so gently they would never tear. Then he would hand me the pole and I would cast my line into the water. I remember how I loved the color and shape of the salmon eggs as they lay all in rows inside the jar. They looked like pink pearls there in the jar and I wanted to have a necklace of them. He said he could make me one but that the eggs wouldn't last that way very long. He said we would come here next summer, but he died and then we never came here again. My mother said that she didn't ever want to come here again.

What do I really remember about him? I keep thinking about that. His blue eyes, his hands, how I liked sitting on his lap, that I loved him in a ten-year-old way. But he is really just a series of images now, the strongest of these found in this place.

We would walk down to the lake to fish, but also to look for the mountain goats you could find along the ledges of the rock in the evening. We would bring the binoculars, and first my grandfather would take them and look until he saw a few tiny white flecks against the rock. Sometimes they would seem to be moving, sometimes they were just the tiniest of spots against the brown rock. Then he would hand the glasses to me and hold them while I looked. It always took a long time for me to see them, even with his holding. My eyes would water from looking so hard and sometimes I didn't see them at all. But he always did.

Last night, just at sunset, we walked down to the lake where I had gone with my grandfather to look for mountain goats. The bear attack happened far down the lake and since they are positive they have killed it, the trail is now considered safe again. But nailed to a tree at the entrance to the trail is a red sign with a drawing of a bear standing wide-mouthed, warning all hikers to use caution. I had never seen one of these signs before but they are everywhere in the park now. My little boy, who has brought his camera, had wanted to take a picture of it, but there wasn't enough light.

We began our descent down the trail and I thought about the sign and the boy and girl sleeping in their tent near the lake. We crossed the footbridge over the stream and stopped to watch the water tumble over the boulders in the creek bed. My little girl threw the branch she had been carrying into the foam and turned to watch it float down the stream. Then we entered the woods, going down, the trail narrowing, undergrowth on each side as we went down, until we came to a clearing, and there was the lake – long, wide, with great monoliths of rock rising from all sides.

It was cooler here. The sun had dropped behind the tallest mountain, shattering the sky. The mountain stood black against the sun. I had wanted to tell the children about my grandfather, about fishing here, about the salmon eggs and the mountain goats. But I listened to the wind in the trees, and thought about bears moving through the undergrowth in the woods behind us and I wanted to go back. It was grey by the lake and darker here next to the woods. Then the sun was gone and only a patch of pale sky showed around the mountain, distinct again, after the blinding of the sun.

"I think we should go back," I said.

The children wanted to stay. My little boy was trying to

skip stones in the water. My little girl had another branch and was making circles in the water.

"We'd better go back," I said again. "It's getting dark." My husband shrugged and led us slowly up the trail. He had been trying to see something through the binoculars. We followed him into the woods.

"Let's hurry up a little," I said. I wanted to hurry, wanted to run. I had to stop the urge to look behind, stop the urge to take the childrens' hands and run up the trail. It seemed that something might be close behind if we didn't hurry. When I was little and had to pass a curtainless window at night, I knew that if I wanted to be safe I must never run past it, certain that my running would draw whatever was outside the window in toward me as I ran. It was getting dark when we reached our cabin. Fifteen minutes from the lake back to the campground. Then safe in the cabin, door bolted, the curtains drawn. Though the cabin was still musty, I closed the windows and locked them. The next morning we heard that someone had seen a bear near the lake, although it was on the other side from us and too far away to tell if it was a grizzly.

The summer I was ten we stayed in one of these cabins. They all look alike, even now, and as old as they seemed then. Just a small square cabin with peeling white paint that from a distance looks almost grey. Each cabin has a small living area in the middle, with a sink, a wood stove, a table and some chairs, and a tiny bedroom on each side. But no bathroom. You still have to walk down the path to the lavatory building for that.

I saw a bear that summer. It was night and I was going down the path to the bathroom. The courtyard was dark except for a pale square of light coming from the cabin across from us. I had my flashlight, and with it I could see only a round circle of light on the path, and my tennis shoes beneath the edge of my nightgown. I heard a dog barking and then there was another sound. Not a growl or a roar, but a deep, heavy sound, unidentifiable and enormous, covering all the night in sound, and I was inside the sound, inside the black sound, inside the open mouth.

I didn't move. Then to my left across the courtyard, I saw a dark shape against the place where the square of light should be. I stood watching the dark shape. It blurred. There was a scraping sound and then in the place where the dark shape had been I could see the square of light again. I ran all the way back to our cabin, dropping the flashlight on the path.

"There was a bear. I heard it," I said. My parents didn't believe me. "It couldn't have been a bear, honey, they stay high in the mountains. They never come down here." They were easterners and bears stayed in the mountains according to the rules.

But my grandfather believed me. The next morning we found that the garbage cans near our cabins had been overturned. Other people had heard something in the night. Something had been there. After breakfast, my grandfather and I measured the distance between where I thought I had been and where I had seen the bear. Twenty big steps. I looked for the bear the rest of the vacation but I never saw him again.

We have learned a lot about bears in the two days we have been here. For one thing, grizzlies aren't circus bears, like the black bears in Yellowstone Park who used to come up to your car or wander into the campgrounds begging for food. Here, in Glacier Park, you hardly ever see bears near the campgrounds or even on the trails. But things are different this hot summer. Now any bear sighting is considered dangerous.

There are three hundred grizzlies (which are brown) and five hundred black bears (which can be either black or brown) in this park that, we are told, holds the largest concentration of grizzlies anywhere in America. We have also learned that the distinction between the two is important because the black bear is smaller than the grizzly and will usually retreat rather than risk a confrontation. He can climb trees, however. The grizzly, on the other hand, is unpredictable and always dangerous, although he is not supposed to be able to climb trees. Which would be better to meet on the trail depends, I suppose, on the size of the trees. A grizzly stands almost nine feet tall and most of the scrub pines on the higher trails aren't much taller than that.

We are told that in the unlikely event we should encounter a bear, we must never attempt to outrun it. One brochure states that if we spotted a bear on a ridge three hundred yards away, it could cover the distance in twenty seconds, if it wanted to. So instead of running you're supposed to move slowly away from the bear, talking softly to it. We laugh, imagining what we would be saying while we moved slowly away from a grizzly bear pawing the air. But if the bear charges anyway, the best protection is to drop to the ground, curl up in a ball and play dead, covering your neck with your hands.

But the worst possible situation is to come suddenly upon bear cubs. They say that a mother bear will do anything to protect them, ignoring her own danger, even when she might safely retreat. So if you drop to the ground and play dead, you're stuck near the cubs; but if you run away, you might excite the mother to frenzy. The only thing to do then is to quickly climb a tree. The pamphlet does not suggest what to do if the only trees available are short ones, or what to do if there are no trees at all.

Everyone in the campground is talking about the bears. Everyone claims they have seen them – on the trails, on the slopes feeding on the berries, on the ridge. My husband thought he saw a bear through his binoculars high up the side of the slope by our cabin. It was just a dark spot along the top of a stretch of green that was there one moment and then gone. He can see things through the binoculars that I can't.

There are bear lectures given by the forest rangers, bear slide shows, bear posters, bear books. My little boy buys a copy of *Night of the Grizzlies* in the gift shop. It was written in 1969 but has again become a best seller here in the park. Something called bear bells are being sold for five dollars a pair. They look more like Santa Claus bells than something that could protect you from bears. They sound like that too. We buy some for our little girl and tie them to her tennis shoes. The sound they make can hardly be heard above the scuffing of her feet on the gravel. But they are great fun for her and she thinks she is invincible. She walks about smugly, stomping her feet in the dust. We even see adults wearing them, laced to their shoes. Tinkle tinkle, they say, as people walk about the campground. I look at their feet and remember the enormous sound I heard in the night a long time ago. But the hikers with the backpacks and wool socks and hiking boots don't wear bear bells.

The local newspapers are still carrying stories of the park board inquest investigating the bear maulings. My little boy searches the paper each morning for articles about it. The paper reports that the boy and the girl who were mauled are the second and third persons to be killed in the park this year. The first was a man who was killed by a grizzly while he was hiking high up on the ridge earlier in the summer. Altogether there have been six reported bear killings in the park's seventy-one year history. Half of them have happened this summer.

My little boy recognizes the word sex in the article.

"What's human sexual activity?" he asks.

I explain.

"Oh, that," he says. He draws the toe of his shoe through the gravel. "But how would that attract the bears?"

I don't know. I have no idea. Noise? Movement? I remember the strange list. "Maybe it's the scent," I say, not thinking.

"The scent of what?" He really wants to know.

"We'll talk about it later, okay?" He looks at me suspiciously then looks away.

It's pretty funny. I can hardly wait to tell his father. I thought about saying something like, "Why don't you go over there and ask that forest ranger?" but I don't because he probably would and I don't want him to be embarrassed. Still, what can he be thinking? In what strange way is he connecting sex and the bloody horror of a bear mauling, whose every gory detail has been described in the papers? I wonder too what there would be about love-making that could provoke such an unexpected and wild thing as this bear mauling? But we have carefully explained to them that the two people who were killed were in a tent not a cabin like ours, that it happened at night, not during the day, and that they have nothing to be afraid of. But they aren't afraid. They are fascinated.

More than the lake, and more than the mountains, even, I want to see the alpine meadows. You can get there easily by taking the Granite Park Chalet trail that leads north of the campground to the pass through the mountains. It is a well-traveled and well-marked trail and not a difficult climb. It is one of the trails that my grandfather and I took that summer. I remember packing sandwiches in pieces of waxed paper and putting them into his knapsack. We didn't carry any water because we were going to drink the water from the mountain streams high up on the trail.

But this summer the rangers are warning people not to drink from the streams because some organism I'd never heard of has been found in the water. It is a parasite that comes from the feces of the mountain goats who live on the top ridges of the mountains and it can make you really sick. But that summer my grandfather and I drank from the streams, drank icy water spilling down over the rocks and pebbles. We just knelt down and used our hands.

It took us half a day to make the climb, going higher and higher up the trail, drinking from the streams higher yet, and eating our sandwiches, finally, at the top on a rock in the middle of a field of flowers. As we climbed, everything got bigger and bigger, the sky next to the snow on the tops of the mountains, the sun white on the snow, and the mountains going out in rows so that you couldn't see if they ever stopped. I thought that we must be looking out at the whole world. And it was wide and beautiful. But it was terrible, too, to be so small standing on the edge of the mountain like that.

And there, at what must have been the very top, were the tiniest flowers I had ever seen, growing in clusters out of the earth and out of the cracks in the rocks — tiny red, orange, yellow, blue flowers. When you first looked at them you just saw them as spots of color, and only by bending down and looking closely could you see how intricate and lovely they were. My ten-year-old hand could have held dozens of them. I lay on my stomach and watched them growing in the sun, rising out of the hard earth and rocks, growing where there were no trees or grass or plants at all. My grandfather explained how they could survive under ten feet of snow all winter to bloom every year for a few weeks in August. He said they were alive under the snow and that even that much winter couldn't kill them.

We were so high, there on the edge of the mountain, that we imagined we could see animals on the ridges of rock above us. We pretended we saw the mountain goats on the ledge beneath the highest ridge, and they weren't white specks through the binoculars, but horns and white bodies and we could see their sharp eyes and the hardness of their hooves.

Then my grandfather said, "There's our bear," and

we pretended that we could see him too, though much further away, standing upright at the very top of the ridge against the sky. And he explained how the bear could live under the winter, too. I remember how my grandfather promised he would bring me back to the meadows again. But he didn't. More than anything else this vacation, I want to go to the alpine meadows. I want to see the flowers, and sit on a rock in the sun. I want to eat my sandwich by the flowers. And I want to drink water from the stream using just my hands.

On the third day, our next to last day here, we take the Granite Park trail. My little boy tells us that the bear attacks in the book happened just the other side of the pass near Granite Chalet. It is non-fiction, he says. He is half-way through the book and tells us that the bear has already killed two girls and is now being hunted down by the forest rangers. He wants to bring the book along, but I make him leave it in the cabin. He brings his camera instead.

It is early morning when we start out, but the sun is high enough to warm the thin, blue air. No clouds in the sky today, only the tops of the mountains. The trail begins easily in the cool, almost chilly wooded stretch, but soon winds its way up so that the piny shade alternates with open rocky stretches of sun. I like the warmth of the open places where I can see ahead and to the sides of the trail. I am a little uneasy in the shady patches where you cannot see what might be moving in the bushes.

The children are excited and walking well. My little girl has her branch and waves it in the air as we go. She stomps her feet to ring the bear bells, but soon gets tired and goes back to scuffing.

To scare away the bears my little boy has put rocks in some pop cans and has strung them to his belt with twine. Clang, clang, tinkle, tinkle. We sound like a Salvation Army band.

The trail is absent of all people this morning, but maybe it is just too early for most hikers. We are the only ones on this stretch of the trail until we pass a man and woman.

"Merry Christmas!" my little boy shouts. The couple are wearing bear bells and they look back at us blankly.

I am a little worried. Maybe we shouldn't carry our food with us, though I know it is packed safely. And we are carrying our own water. Maybe we shouldn't be doing this at all. I have the feeling that it is really all right and that it is also incredibly foolish.

I listen and watch for any dark movement in the bushes or on the brown slopes ahead. The trail goes up the side of the mountain and to the right we see the sharp, upward slope, and to the left the slope down, which is wooded and impenetrable. We descend through a dark stretch of pine; it turns sharply left, and then unexpectedly opens up to the valley below. For the first time we can see how really high we are, and we look down and feel how wild and high this is. We can see the lake and it looks small surrounded by the mountains. We can see the way the timber grows dense and green near the lake, then brown in between the green places farther on, then straight up layers and layers of rock.

My little boy takes a picture. "It's beautiful," he says.

The sun is on everything, on the water, on the mountain peaks, on the tops of the trees below, on the trail, on our shoulders. It is so lovely it seems impossible for a bear to be here. But it is high enough, I am thinking. We have done very well to come this far, we should go back now. We haven't seen anyone on the trail since the couple wearing the bear bells.

"Do you think we should keep going?" I say.

"Why not?" my husband asks.

"It's still pretty far to the top."

Everyone wants to keep going. My husband puts my little girl on his shoulders. "Keep the branch out of my eyes," he says as he lifts her up. She drops the branch and holds onto his face.

It must seem very high sitting five feet higher than the ground, so close to the edge. Tinkle tinkle go the bells as her feet bounce with his steps.

My husband isn't worried, he thinks we are fine. He leads the way, the children between us, me in back. I am tired, not from walking, but from the responsibility of watching. I am the only one who is really watching, I think. I cannot believe that just staying on the trails will keep us safe. How could a bear know what a trail is? Maybe if the children weren't with us. I could never protect them. They would run all in different directions and I couldn't keep us together. I would do anything to save them, but what could I do? I'm not big enough to cover them or be their shelter even if I could keep them from running. Maybe if I just felt safer in this wild place. It is so big and it has no boundaries or rules that I know.

But the children are delighted. They are laughing and singing, hoping to see a bear somewhere up the slope.

Who's afraid of the big bad bear, they sing.

It is getting hot and my husband has taken off his shirt. His brown back shines in the sun. I have my sweatshirt tied around my waist and can feel the sun burn onto my back too. My little girl is walking beside me, holding my hand, sucking her thumb. My little boy has run on ahead, has turned the corner out of sight. The sky is everywhere.

"I wish he wouldn't do that," I say.

"Do what?"

"Run on ahead like that. I can't see where he is."

"He's all right," my husband says.

"I know he's all right, I just don't like him running off like that."

"I want to run off too," my little girl says, looking up at me. But she doesn't let go of my hand.

The couple who passed us must be far below by now. There are no other hikers on this trail. I know that the two people were killed at night, in the dark, through the canvas. Not in the sun, not during the day. But there was no reason for it, no sense to it or provocation.

"I think we should go back," I say.

"Why? The children are fine."

"She'll never be able to make it to the top," I say, knowing that it isn't true.

"I'll carry her the rest of the way."

"I really think we should go back."

"But you wanted to see the flowers. This is important to you." It is not my daughter's fatigue and he knows it. We turn the corner and I can see my little boy up ahead.

He has climbed onto a rocky ledge up the slope, and he's standing on top, taking our picture. "Smiiile!" he yells.

"See? He's all right," my husband says.

"This is just crazy," I say. I can feel the panic catch in my throat.

"Look at him," my husband says. He knows what I am thinking. "Can't you see he's all right? They cured him, for godsake." I watch him climb down off the rocks, careful not to bang the camera swinging from his neck, then he's running toward us, and the pop cans at his waist make the only sound. He sees us just stopped there in the middle of the trail. He tells me that I shouldn't worry about the bears. He knows what I am thinking, too.

"It's all right, Mom. We'll scare them away." He rattles the pop cans. "It's okay, isn't it, Dad?" I look at them. And then at my little girl.

"I'm going back," I say. I know that this will end it, that we will all go back now. We haven't seen the flowers, we haven't eaten our lunch, we haven't even come high enough to reach the mountain streams.

We turn and go down. Nobody says anything. The singing stops. No sounds now but the tinkle tinkle from the bells on my little girl's shoes and the occasional clanging of the pop cans. I lead the way, so they cannot see that I am crying.

It doesn't take us very long to follow the trail down to camp. Now we see other hikers on the trail. Several groups of them pass us on their way up to the meadows. It is barely noon when we reach the cabin. We eat our sandwiches on the table inside. It is the last day before we have to go home. In the morning we take a boat tour of the lake.

There are thirty of us in the covered launch, and a forest ranger who points out the scenic spots as we circle the lake. I look at the woods and the mountains through the window of the boat. A group of people are on horseback far up the side of the mountain. I watch them through the window of the boat. They are so high and so far away it is difficult at first to tell that they are moving. An eagle soars. The ranger points him out, identifies it.

At the upper end of the lake we get out of the boat and the ranger leads us into the woods for a hike up to the waterfalls. I think this is the side of the lake where it happened. But they wouldn't bring a *tour* here, not if this really were the place. And anyway, the bear is dead.

We go very slowly, thirty of us in single file. The ranger stops every so often to identify a plant species. But all of the plants here are big and leafy and green and there are so many people in front of us that we can't see what he is describing. At the waterfalls there is a wood railing which we do not go beyond. We wait our turn to stand by the railing and look at the waterfall. It is cool and dark here and it is pleasant to look at it, as we have heard the water rushing for some time. The rest of the people are below us, getting down the trail. We are the last to leave and we have the trail to ourselves for the hike back to the boat.

There is a stone in my shoe and I sit down in the middle of the trail to take it out. I watch my husband and my little girl on his shoulders, bobbing up and down, as he makes his way down the trail. My little boy has run on ahead. It takes a turn and they all disappear. It is green everywhere, on both sides of the trail, green where the sky is. I sit on the ground and listen to the green silence.

If there were a bear I would hear it way before I could ever see it. If it were moving, and not just still and waiting. I would hear the dark shape coming through the green, but I would never be able to see it in time. I would never have time to stand up, time only to cover my neck with my hands. I put my shoe on, hurrying the laces. Looking straight ahead at the trail going down, I make myself walk as far as the turn. Then I run all the rest of the way, my shoelaces flopping in the dirt. They are waiting for me in the boat. I am glad to see the boat rocking in the water, and the sky again, and the mountains where the horses are.

In the afternoon we drive into Canada. It is late in the afternoon when we get back to the cabin. The children say they are ready to go home, that they miss their friends. The pop cans lie in a heap outside the door of the cabin.

In the evening, we drive a few miles out of the park to the big hotel for dinner. Afterwards my husband takes the children to a wildlife slide show. I drive the car back to the campground.

I need to begin packing and I do not want to see any more pictures of Glacier Park. The cabin is hot and stuffy and I open the windows. I begin to pack my little girl's things. I pack the Indian doll her father bought for her our first day here. I look at it lying in the bottom of the suitcase and remember going to the gift shop, my vacation money wilting in my hand, looking at everything, looking at the polished agates and the Indian beads and the silver rings. But more than anything I had wanted white Indian moccasins, the kind with soft, silent soles and colored beads. I decide to go to the gift shop to find a pair that might fit our four-year-old daughter.

The sun has gone from behind the mountain. I still wear my dinner clothes and sandals and the evening feels cool on my skin. I start off toward the gift shop, thinking about the Indian moccasins, but find that I have somehow gotten off the path. Instead, I follow the trail that goes past the footbridge, past the stream, past the red sign tacked to the tree, down through the undergrowth, down, down, then straight down through the trees and into a clearing, and to the lake. To look at the water and the mountains, I imagine, and to watch for mountain goats, and to think about my grandfather.

I sit on a log by the water, looking at nothing in particular. I am cold in my dress and sandals. I do not look behind into the woods. I sit and sit, waiting for a rustling sound, the sound something heavy would make moving from side to side through the bushes. I know that I haven't come here to see the water or the mountain goats or to think about my grandfather. I have come to wait for the bear. I have come to wait for the bear at last. But the air is empty and I hear only the high, light sound of the wind in the trees. I will sit here for a while, and if he does not come, I will make my way back to camp and begin packing, for in the morning we are going home.

The Wheelman

Beverly Conner

When the world embarked on a new millennium that most folks took to be the year 2000 – a year predicted to bring great or maybe cataclysmic change – it also happened that Tyler and Alicia McConnell lost their only child. After that, with hardly a pause to catch his breath, Ty's life skidded around a blind corner, and for a year it looked as if his parts might never be put right. Then slowly the frame was raised and repairs made, but none of it happened fast enough to save his marriage. And Ty had to admit it was his own collision with Derek's death more than Ali's rolling grief that pulled her away from him. Or him from her. To her credit she had sought out friends, talked to a minister, found a support group for parents who had lost children – people who, unlike Ty, could bear the articulation of ever-fresh grieving.

Because Derek had been a big and sturdy three-year-old, they had enrolled him in a gymnastics-for-toddlers preschool class. Not because of any particular athletic aptitude but just to burn off some energy in a kid who'd given up naps before he turned two, who had all his shots, swallowed daily vitamins, and suffered fewer than a handful of colds his whole young life. When Ali was pregnant, they agreed she would stay home with Derek the first couple of years to give him a good start, and she hadn't minded a break from the Seattle real estate office where she and Ty had met.

Road bikers since their teens, they bought a tandem bike with a trailer to pull Derek along behind, zipping up his parka and fastening his small yellow helmet before a morning ride through the Burke Gilman Trail, sometimes passing the University of Washington, other days stopping to picnic at GasWorks Park.

As many anxieties as parents might conjure in those morning-gray hours before birdsong, neither of them ever imagined the word *meningitis*, let alone the sky-high temperature, the lumbar punctures, the ICU, their baby boy dead within two days. And no experimental drug, no white-coated healer, no miracle of faith or blessed grace had kept Derek with them.

The graveside ceremony was private. Alicia's parents flew up from Los Angeles; Ty's parents, frail in Minnesota, sent flowers that dwarfed the small coffin. Derek Lee McConnell, born May 5, 1997 (their *Cinco de Mayo* baby), died June 4, 2000.

When Derek was born, Ty brought a piñata to the hospital along with a bouquet of Irises – Ali's favorite – mixed with baby's breath because he liked the name. Ali saved the piñata – a red and orange parrot – for Derek's first birthday when he was still too small to bash it open himself. They hadn't wanted him to think it nifty to go around slamming things with a big stick. So Ty blindfolded Ali, which seemed a little sexy after a Margarita or maybe they'd had two, and she whacked the piñata hard enough to explode small wrapped candies across the floor. Too late they realized the choking potential of the treats, so Ali diverted Derek with a handful of miniature marshmallows on his high chair tray while Ty swept away the little bright dangers. As he emptied the dustpan, he didn't guess that Derek would regularly demand marshmallows for the next two months. But he figured rightly that he and Ali would make love that night.

After Derek's death, Ali picked up a new vocabulary from counselors that she passed on to Ty in an attempt to help or maybe just to shake him out of the black canyon into which he fell. Depression, suppression, denial, complicated grief, or his personal favorite of the bunch: Grief Displacement Disorder. No shit.

A prescription for anti-depression medication flattened him. When the doctor suggested trial-and-adjustment were involved in these meds, Ty dumped the pills, cancelled his next appointment, and took to the road.

He didn't invite Ali along, even though she was easily fit enough for the 50-mile bike rides that quickly stretched to 100 and soon took up every spare hour outside work. His commissions suffered but in view of the death in the family, the firm cut him some slack.

Against the back wall of the garage, a well-meaning neighbor had thrown a sheet over the tandem and its trailer, but Ali eventually pulled it off. She said it looked like a shroud, and he didn't know if she meant for their baby or their marriage – or both at once.

He bought new bike lights and reflective gear and began to ride after dark, a riskier hour they'd both avoided after Derek was born. He missed dinners at home, carrying water and protein bars he bought by the score from Costco. Many mornings before work he pedaled off for a long ride leaving Ali still in bed. He noticed she seemed to be sleeping more lately. So let her take those damned pills.

He put on muscle but lost weight. They stopped having people over for dinner, and after the post-funeral condolences, friends kept a little distance. After all, he was seldom available. A fellow agent invited him to join the local Wheelman's Bicycle club, but Ty wanted no part of their socializing banter.

Finally he was persuaded to sign up for The 2001 Courage Classic, a three-day ride in August over three passes in the Cascade Mountains to raise money for the local children's hospital. Derek had been gone for just over a year. Ty didn't have the heart to turn down an event to help other people's kids, but neither did he mention it to Ali in time for her to register for the event, let alone train.

On the morning of the ride, Ali rose early to drop him off in North Bend where the riders gathered. Along the way, they stopped for lattes, more for her than for him with his pre-ride jitters. Neither one said much. When she pulled the car up to the drop-off area, Ty jumped out quickly to hoist his beetle-green bike off the rack.

She rolled down the car window. "Have a good ride," she said, and it sounded to him very close to have a good life. He remembered a couple years back when he bought the outfit he was wearing: the Day-Glo chartreuse bike shirt, the tight black biker shorts. She'd said then he looked like a sexy grasshopper. It didn't seem to matter now, to either of them. He leaned down to kiss her lightly before turning away.

The event had no start time, no gun going off. By 7 A.M. a disc jockey was playing music through a powerful sound system. People pulled bikes off cars, filled tires, kissed spouses, and high-five'd their kids. A service club handed out coffee and muffins. Riders took off once they got their numbers fastened like bibs to handlebars and to the backs of their bike seats. Each rider sported an elastic-ribbed helmet cover as further proof of registration and wore a plastic wristband that served as a food ticket.

Elite cyclists rode ten or so bikers in a pace line, pedals going in sync; some of them planned to make all three passes in one day, maybe 10 hours, about 172 miles. But except for the pace lines, most bikers spread out, with some riding in groups for company and encouragement. Each day on the long uphill grades was a test of strength and endurance, first to Snoqualmie Summit, then Blewett Pass, and finally the last day's ride over Steven's Pass. The goal was simply to finish – no one was timed – and to collect pledges for the hospital. For the kids, Ty thought – the three words becoming a mantra as he rode. His co-workers had pledged over $500 in Derek's name, all the money going to the hospital.

Behind Ty rode husbands and wives, teenagers, retired people, teams from businesses or service clubs like Rotary, and a few folks who looked like they might not make the first dozen miles. At designated rest stops, volunteers handed out snacks, sports drinks and water, and by as early as 11:30 they were giving out fat, plastic-wrapped sandwiches. Tubes of sunscreen were handy for those who forgot the hazards of high, bright air when they had packed up their gear in the early-morning mists of the I-5 corridor. First-aid kits were set by for blisters or spills or bike chain scrapes. "Sag Wagons" roamed from front-rider to straggler and back, toting baggage and water, offering lifts for rider and bike to anyone getting too tired. In mid-afternoon, one Rotary club handed out hot-fudge sundaes from a refrigerated truck.

Always among the first 75 or so riders to finish and roll into the designated park or school athletic field, on the second day at Leavenworth Ty skipped the apprentice masseurs set up to offer riders massages for a buck a minute. Famished, he quickly got in line to scarf down the hearty chili and foil-wrapped baked potatoes, the fresh-sliced oranges and homemade Brownies served up by volunteers who cheered him along the food line as if he were still riding the course:

Attaboy!

Keep 'er goin', tiger!

Almost halfway! Legs holdin' up?

And from a silver-haired woman handing out hot cornbread and foil-wrapped pats of butter: *You are just a darlin' boy!* Really? Could she not see his 37 years, or was every rider coming through the food line some kind of darlin' in her eyes?

After dinner and the day's stories, many riders spread sleeping bags on floors of shared motel rooms, but Ty avoided as much conversation as he could. Along with a few families who pretty much kept to themselves, he camped out in the designated city parks in his bedroll both nights. Most of the motels had been booked long ago anyway, the streets oddly empty of the usual weekend cars, the bikers taking over one town and then another.

On the last day riding the 74 miles over Steven's Pass – the most grueling of the three – Ty was skimming the asphalt on a long and welcome downhill grade, not really going for speed but not reining it in either. The high-altitude air was hot and dry, a perfect late-summer day, and his skin glowed from windburn, his chest softened by a rare tranquility. The road was wide and sweeping – a safe coast down.

Into that uncommon peace, like a flash of dry lightning, the absence of his son's future pleasures struck him an electrifying blow: how Derek would never breathe fir-scented air or lick wind-parched lips, never know the heart-deep abundance his father had felt just seconds ago.

Ty shifted the bike to a higher gear to outpace pain, as if he ever could, the trees a green smear in his peripheral vision. He might have been up to forty miles an hour, the road stretching down and ahead towards a bend to the left that he reached swiftly. Without slowing he leaned into the curve, the angle of bike and rider so familiar, a kind of comfort in this one competence.

Suddenly, no more than twenty yards ahead, a line of at least a dozen riders was halted, each taking a turn at a stop sign that came out of nowhere. Or he'd missed the warning of it, distracted by thoughts of Derek. His calculations were swift, born of the miles he and the bike had logged. He could pass the others on their left, trusting no traffic was coming on Highway 2, a dangerous gamble. Or he could slam on his brakes, no way to know if he could stop in time, yet it seemed the better gamble. He pushed back on his seat to throw his weight toward the rear, but what he couldn't calculate was the scattering of slippery Doug fir needles and soft gravel thrown up by braking trucks on the approach to the highway stop sign.

He gripped his hand brakes, and as they seized his tires, he slid over gravel spread like glass petals beneath him, his bike leaning into the road, the flesh of his bare right arm and leg peeling off against the asphalt as he skidded toward the riders, body and bike veering onto the shoulder at the last moment to avoid slamming into the group. His bike somersaulted down the embankment as he was lifted clear of the seat. In that odd mid-air clarity as he flew across the ditch, he could not be sure his body would miss the stand of maples that flanked the other side. He tried to tuck and roll and smashed onto the ground two feet from the nearest tree.

After that the details were fuzzy. His bike lay like a crumpled insect beneath the sky. An Aid Car took him down to the hospital. Another biker fished his cell phone out of his pannier, and when they were finally out of the mountains, Ty called Ali, telling her he'd had a problem with his bike, he was okay, but he needed her to meet him at the ER. Someone trucked what was left of his bike down the mountain and kindly delivered it to their front porch, the frame bent beyond repair. The wheels were taco'd – bent so nearly in half they were ruined.

Three nurses worked him over, scrubbing with brushes the road burn and the abrasions that ran deeper, scrubbing with disinfectant and picking gravel out of deep cuts. They were kind, apologetic for the pain. Ty tried to smile as one patted his shoulder. They applied burn dressings to the worst of the wounds, gave him antibiotics, told him to take extra-strength acetaminophen when he got home, to drink plenty of water because of shock.

Turned out his helmet was cracked, which meant somewhere, trees or otherwise, he had hit his head. He didn't want the CAT scan. Shock, they told him, even when he insisted he was fine, you're in shock so we need to check you out, and they put him in a wheelchair and rolled him down the hall to that big white tube in Radiology. Hop onto the platform, the technician who looked young as a boy told him, but when they saw his shoulders tremble, they said again it was shock and you're not claustrophobic, are you? They helped him, laid him back and slid him in, told him to lie still.

Inside that domed steel coffin, it wasn't claustrophobia that rushed at him but a wave of anger black as swamp water, a rage that overturned the boggy grief he'd sealed off in some place these long months. He began to shake and they asked him again to hold still please, and he was suddenly afraid because he wanted to kill someone – anyone in a mocking white doctor-coat or scrubs because all this attention and technology and skill, all this fucking medicine hadn't saved one small boy.

But he managed to lie still while the scan ticked away, managed because he was startled by slow tears leaking down past his ears, puddling beneath his head. And their slow rivulets – sweet Jesus! – his tears tickled. He clenched his fists, not in anger, but to stifle laughter at this latest absurdity: in the face of tragedy, dear god, he itched. He remembered that country song from years back, "I've Got Tears in My Ears from Lying on My Back Crying over You." Ali never believed it was a real song, said he made it up to tease her.

He wondered whether a CAT scan could detect a man's tears, or a flash of heat to the brain, or an impulse toward harsh laughter that might signal nothing more than a good knock in the noggin. But truth was he didn't really give a rat's ass. When they rolled him out, the young technician leaned over him without a word and wiped his face with a wad of cotton.

Be sure to have someone pick you up, they said. You're in no condition to drive. But he'd already called Ali to come get him. He was pretty sure he had.

To his wife in the waiting room with her car keys clutched in a damp hand, they said he seems okay, but keep an eye on him, especially watch for lethargy or sleeping too much or a heaviness in his legs. A closed head injury could make him foggy; it has to be taken seriously. Ty didn't think either of them were exactly celebrating.

Afterward Ali said he was slightly glassy-eyed but that didn't seem much different to her from the past few months, and where was this death wish going to get him anyway? It wasn't as if he'd killed their child.

But he hadn't saved him either. And how long a road would it take to ride away from that?

I Guard The White Rhino

Hans Ostrom

First you must know that the white rhinoceros isn't white. Its hide is brownish gray. Its massive lower jaw, however, is *wider* than the jaw of the black rhinoceros. Somehow *wide* became *white* in English. Such confusion must happen all the time in that language.

Then you must know that I, Joseph Natal, have always wanted to be a park ranger. By saying "always," I'm exaggerating but only just. My father, a baker in Nairobi, wanted me to bake, or to drive a bakery truck. But by the time I was nine years old, I had dreams – plans – to roam the savannas amongst the great beasts. "Might as well have been born with a spear in your hand," said my father, who meant the comment as an insult, for he'd grown up in Nairobi. I just smiled.

The joke was on me. I became a ranger, all right, but I don't roam the savannas or any other place. I hardly move. I guard the white rhino.

For years poachers have slaughtered rhinos all over

Africa and Asia – the black ones, the white ones, the Javans, the Sumatrans. They kill all kinds. Why? To leave them in a rotting heap, three tons – three metric tons, I tell you – of meat and bone in one animal, decaying in dirt, caked in flies. You see, they want only the horn, to grind up for love-powder, "aphrodisiac." It doesn't do anything, this powder. I, Joseph Natal, tried it once. My wife asked, "Why do you just lie there?" "I'm waiting," I said. "For what?" she said. "For the rhino powder to overwhelm me and turn me into a beast," I said. "Forget the powder, silly child," she said, "and get over here."

In South Africa, they can spend much money to fence their big parks and send rangers in swarms to ward off if not arrest the poachers. Here in Kenya, no such fortune. Can't fence the big parks, not many rangers, more rhinos perish.

So there's a little fenced park out here, nowhere, hot as hell, and we have 23 white rhinos we hope will make more rhinos. Twenty-three means four *crashes*. A *crash* is a group of approximately six rhinos, not a family but something like it.

They're buildings, these rhinos. Legs like marble pillars, I tell you. Each one weighs more than my house! Jomo and Robert and I guard them, round the clock, every day and night. Jomo and I – moody Robert takes the night shift – lean against them, bounce pebbles off their hides, scratch their tough, rubbery ears: we are like flies to them. They don't know we guard them. We are part of the world that annoys them.

So boring for us. To stand and stand and stand. To walk about. The big challenge is to avoid the dung heaps.

Something in the rhinos' brains tells them to mark territory with massive communal dung heaps and ponds of urine. Our small fences are nothing to them. They could blast through if they wanted to. The fences are for the poachers. The rhinos could also trample us to death whenever they wanted to. But they've grown used to us. They tolerate us. We're no surprise, no threat.

It is so tedious to watch over these building-animals. Better to be a baker than a janitor for rhinos! My father was right. I carry a rifle, not a spear.

Sometimes, though, I stare at their big, sad, folded skin, and at their heads, heavy as truck-cabs, and at the enormous spike of bone that gets them in so much trouble. I stare and I think I can see back centuries, millennia. I look at that tiny black eye surrounded by a savanna of hide, and I think sometimes it's God's eye. The eye is like a portal to lost eons. I have not told this to Jomo, or to Robert. They might report me, say I'm crazy, say the job has done me in. Maybe it has.

At other times, when the day's heat is relenting and shadows stretch long over grass, and the wind blows through leaves, I look over at that head that's been munching and snuffling and snorting since forever on this plain, and I think, what if I'm guarding gods? What does that head really know? It could know everything. Everything. It could know how old exactly the rhino species are and remember dinosaurs.

No, of course I don't let on I think these things. I curse the stinking shit-piles, just like Jomo does, and why not? When a three-ton animal that eats all day lets loose in the sun and heat and the wind blows in your face, you know it, brother.

I laugh when they copulate, one truck on top of another. Good Lord, the grunting! Then eight months later, out drives a small truck.

I complain about the job and plan with Jomo to buy a ranch.

The last time I saw one the poachers had got, dead in the dirt just outside the enclosure, I cried like my daughter. Its huge forlorn buttocks were as still as boulders. Big bullet holes gaped in its sides, and there was more blood in the dust than I could believe. The horn was sawed off. A scandalous sight. All the rest was beginning to rot – to rot, for nothing. Jomo said, "What's wrong, brother? You've seen this before." I walked away. I couldn't explain.

And now sometimes when I go home at night and lift up my daughter and kiss her, she seems as light as a flower. She weighs nothing, and I get scared. I feel like nothing. My house seems like paste-board, and everything we own seems like a joke, and I think again that maybe the rhinos and elephants know everything. We ride them and bounce rocks off them and shoot them down for ivory and powder, and they just seem to wait – not a family but something like it. The great beasts. The noble ones. They seem to take everything we can give, and the ones left alive go back to munching and wallowing in mud and conducting their bluff-fights. I think they know they just have to wait, and – *poof* – we'll be gone.

I tell this to my wife, and she says, "You stand in the sun too much. Rhinos are big stupid animals, O.K.?"

I say, "All right," and I calm down and play with my daughter and have dinner like before and the house feels sturdy. Then at night I have a bad dream, rhinos thundering across the savanna, millions of three-toed hooves smashing the ground, heading for Nairobi. Trees fall over. Then I'm in the way. The sun goes dark, and the horn comes for me, and I jump awake, sweating, breathing like I've been running.

My wife says, "What's the matter? Settle down."

I blurt out, "I wonder if Robert is dead."

She says, "Robert? Robert isn't dead. Your job's making you crazy, Joseph. Lie back down."

I lie down. But I'm wide awake all night. *Wide.* I tell myself, "They're big and stupid and they defecate all day and night and they roll in the mud. They are not like family, not even almost." But down in me a belief persists that maybe they are gods. Either way, I'm going to guard them well. It is my job, after all. I think I'll throw dried mud at them instead of rocks. And if it comes to where I need guarding, maybe they'll remember. Brother, sister: I hope so.

In Another Country

Ann Putnam

"What's this?" I said to Jay, who was watching Monday Night Football, stretched out on the easy chair. We all called it the dental chair because when you leaned all the way back you looked like you were having your teeth drilled. I came into the family room holding the envelope from the Tumor Institute. I'd found it on the dining room table lying benignly enough in between the bills and junk ads.

"Go ahead and read it," Jay said from the chair.

The letter was just a gentle reminder for Jay to please make an appointment for his next CAT scan, but my heart was pounding. I sat down and dropped the letter in my lap. I kept looking at that letterhead. Jay was watching the game.

"I didn't know all this would be so soon," I said.

"Every six months. I told you."

"For how long."

"I don't know, a while."

"God, Jay, how long is a while?"

"I don't know, a while. How do I know?"

"Why do they need to do this again, anyway?"

"I suppose it's to see if it's come *back*" Jay said, finally looking up from the TV.

"Well, you never told me."

"Sure I did. You just don't remember." He glared at me.

"You didn't, though," I said, softer this time. I was leaving in the morning for Texas and neither of us wanted a quarrel.

Jay went back to the football game. He looked weary to me. It was over the hump night and we'd all made it through the first half of the week, but in that light I thought he looked weary. But so what? On Wednesday night everybody looks tired.

I'd watched him all those months for signs of recovery or relapse. What could a test tell me that I couldn't see for myself? Wouldn't his eyes or the sound of his voice tell us more than that? Tonight, though, stretched out like that he looked like somebody's patient. I wished he'd prop the chair back up and sit up straight. I was beginning to see things in my head. We were entering that inner world again, where cells and nodes and bone and blood would rise up out of the fog, like a developing photograph to tell us what we already knew or what we already feared.

"Jay?" I said.

"Yeah?" His eyes were following the play on the screen.

"I wish I didn't have to go." I sat down in his lap and the chair popped back up.

"I know, but it'll be good for you to get away," he said, trying to convince me not to cancel my reservations and fax my paper for somebody else to read.

"No it won't."

"Sure it will. You should go. The sun will be good for you,"

"No it won't."

"Sure it will," he said, putting his hand under my shirt.

"Okay okay okay," I said, grinning back. "If the plane doesn't crash."

"Just be sure to take out lots of flight insurance," he said, back to the football game again. "We'll be all right."

I put my head in the crook of his neck. I could tell he was watching the football game over the top of my head.

I got up and went over to the refrigerator where I'd tacked up lists for everything. Dog instructions, kid instructions, vet number, emergency vet number, house, carpool, flight numbers, my hotel number. It was all too much trouble. Somebody else could read my paper. But I always said that before every conference I'd ever gone to. Anyway, I'd never been to Texas before.

I got out the atlas and found Dallas on the map. It looked far away. In another country.

I went back into the kitchen to check the rice and hamburger I was cooking for the dog. I wanted to make enough to last the four days I'd be gone. She hadn't eaten anything the past couple of days, so I thought if I made a fresh batch it might tempt her to give it a try. This morning I'd had to help her off the front porch, but she just took a couple of steps and lay down in the gravel in the middle of the driveway. I couldn't remember when I'd last seen her relieve herself. I knew her kidneys had pretty much all but stopped now, knew my rice pottage and antibiotics three times a day weren't going to help much longer. But she'd long ago resigned herself to pills being shoved down her throat, and would open wide every time.

"I'm surprised she's still with us," the vet had said on Monday. I'd gone to pick up another bottle of antibiotics. We were standing in the middle of the waiting room, discussing what do if Niki died over the weekend. Nobody in that room had to lean forward to hear what we were saying. Even the receptionist stopped what she was doing to listen.

"Do you think she can she live another week? I hate to ask, but I'll be gone over the weekend, and I don't really want my husband left alone with all this."

"Looking at these blood counts, I'm surprised she isn't dead already."

Jerk! What did he care? We were no longer an interesting case for some heroic, journal-worthy new procedure. To him all this was just the end of a long slow process, too boring for too long.

"Well, I think we should find out why this happened – I mean, if she could have passed anything on to the pups."

"Then we'll need to go ahead and autopsy the kidneys."

"I know."

"So," he was explaining, "if she dies over the weekend, and I hate to put it this way, you'll need to figure out some way to preserve her, then bring her in on Monday."

I looked over at the little white-haired woman with half a basset hound in her lap, the other half draped across the vinyl couch where they were sitting. She looked at me and blinked and looked away. But I didn't blink, I just charged right on ahead.

"So how do we do that, exactly?"

"Well," he said, lowering his voice. I think he'd just realized he had a waiting room full of people listening to the gory last details of what was obviously a veterinary failure.

He leaned close. "You could put her in the freezer," he said half under his breath.

"What did you say?"

He cleared his throat. "People have done that."

"But she's a big dog."

"Well, I know. But I don't know what else to tell you."

"But how would she fit?"

"Well." He glanced around the room, smiled a fast smile, and edged back toward the reception desk. He was almost in a whisper now. "You take out the food and a couple of shelves and then you can lift her right in." The white-haired woman was getting up off the couch and heading for the door, dragging that basset hound behind her.

It was all pretty funny that Monday afternoon standing in the square of light coming in through the long curtainless window, the umpteenth bottle of antibiotics in my hand.

"We could put her to sleep now. We could have done that weeks ago."

"Yes, I know that, but you said she wouldn't be in any pain."

He just looked at me. Who needed this extra time, I wondered? Who needed the time to get ready for this?

Jay'd wanted to put her down a week ago. What about Niki, what was she holding on for? Maybe she'd wanted to just wander off into the woods some night and lie down for good. Maybe she was sticking around for us. Today she couldn't even get to the front yard.

I scooped up the rice and stuffed it into a big Tupperware container. I snapped the lid shut and put it on the bottom shelf of the refrigerator. Niki looked up at me from the floor where she was lying, trying to get as much of herself as she could under the dishwasher door, left open now most of the time because it had become her favorite place in the kitchen.

"You'll be okay," I said, sitting down on the floor beside her. I lifted up the door so I could give her a hug. She nosed at the bagel I offered her and turned her head. No thank you, not today. I picked up her front paw. It smelled like popcorn, just like always. She rolled over on her back and I rubbed her belly. She still felt like a big stuffed animal. "I'll be back soon," I said. You hold on. She watched me with a bright, fierce look. There was no dulled, glazed-over look here. What did she know after all, I wondered?

I could see the lights of the airport shuttle floating through the morning fog as it worked its uncertain way up our hill. Maybe the airport was fogged in, it was always hard to tell from up here. But I couldn't get through to check. Part of me was hoping the airport was socked in for good. The shuttle pulled up into the driveway and the driver got out and grabbed my luggage from the front porch and headed back to the van.

"See you," I said to Niki. She turned her head away,

and would not look back. She always knew when I was leaving, always knew what that suitcase meant, and when I came back always told me how mad she was I'd gone away. In the middle of the night she'd creep upstairs in search of my overnight bag or my purse. She'd drag one or the other into the living room and dump it all out. In the morning I'd find her outside on the back deck, in despair and ready for sentencing, and the contents of my bag spread out all over the living room.

Once I called the poison control center because I'd found an empty, tooth-marked prescription bottle under the coffee table, no pills anywhere. She sat stoically on the deck, as close to the door as she could get, while I poured half a cup of hydrogen peroxide down her throat according to the directions given by the poison control operator, to induce vomiting that never came. So I'd be sitting in the living room, telling everybody about my trip, and I'd catch her looking at me sideways, through narrowed eyes. Ah, I remember now that you left me.

I grabbed my raincoat out of the closet and looked over at her curled up in the corner of the living room. Good-bye good-bye good-bye, I said, and closed the door.

The wind blew hot and dry across the golf course and the patio where I was sitting next to the swimming pool. That Texas sun hung low and spiteful in the late afternoon sky, flickering in hot, wavering light off the blue-tiled swimming pool. I shut my eyes. If I had to be here, I'd turn my face to the sun, go back a couple of months and pretend it was summer all over again. It was still cold and foggy when the plane left Seattle. I'd sat in the airport for two hours waiting for the fog to clear before we could take off. Well, this was Texas, all right. Everything felt out of season. I guess there was no going back, once you'd made the turn toward winter. Anyway, this was a light not to be trusted.

I was gathering courage to go back inside and find the conference registration table, pick up my name tag, begin the wearying process of what I had supposedly come here for – panels, symposiums, sessions, papers. So what are you working on? Me?

Oh, well. I'm working on just holding things together. My father's sick, the dog is dying, who knows about my husband, but how about you, now how are you? In-your-face kind of stuff. Couldn't we speak our sorrows instead, I wanted to say, and offer comfort in some small way? But of course nobody ever did.

I lay that night in the king-size bed, huddled next to the edge of what would forever be my side of the bed. I'd tried the center of that big bed but there was too much room for comfort. I'd wanted a tight, little unambiguous single bed pressed against the wall. First nights away from home were always disorienting anyway. But it was what I always looked forward to, thinking about it at home in the middle of everything. A room of my own – a bath anytime I wanted, take a book in there, hey, read the whole thing, watch any TV channel, order room service, maybe even get some writing done. Nobody wanting anything. Hours stretching out slow and easy. But it never quite worked out that way. Having no practice at solitude, I always began missing everybody the minute it got dark.

I thought I was never going to fall asleep until the phone woke me up and I reached over to grab it, and rolled right out of bed, knocking the phone off the bedstand onto the floor. So here it was. The phone call in the middle of the night. My heart closed up like a flower in the dark. I sat on the floor while it grew tight and hard inside my chest. If this was it, well, I was ready. I fumbled around on the floor till I found the phone, and lifted it to my ear.

"Hello?" I whispered.

"I wanna fuck you, baby," a voice slurred in my ear.

"What?"

"I wanna fuck your brains out."

I slammed down the receiver. My heart was all over the place, my secret heart open wide and waiting to be wrenched out of my chest after all. I sat there panting. I wasn't ready for anything.

I called the desk.

"Room 411 just got a very disgusting obscene phone call."

"We're terribly sorry about that," some frayed voice sighed back in my ear. "We've got three floors of ROTC officers who've had way too much to drink and we're about ready to boot them all out."

I could hear them now. They were jamming something against my door. It sounded like they were trying to shove a mattress through the doorway but forgot the door was shut.

"You've got the wrong room, you idiots!" I yelled through the door. I looked through the peephole. I could see what looked like the back of somebody's head.

I heard the mattress banging against the door as they got it turned around. I looked at the clock. Two-thirty.

The noises went on down the hall. I went to the bathroom, got a glass of water, took it back to bed, and turned off the light. I could hear somebody using the ice dispenser across the hall, so I put one of the pillows over my head. I thought about everybody back home, wondered if they were safely asleep, and imagined them all — my parents asleep under the white, winter comforter, my father curled up on his right side, a pillow between his bony knees, Jay sleeping on his back his arms across his chest, Niki curled up on my side of the bed, where she always slept when I was gone, Jillie and Max and Will in a tangle of sheets and blankets, their faces warm and flushed with dreams. I'd spread my incantations over them all — a wide, drowsy net of words drifting up through the dark, silent rooftop of the hotel.

I lay there, but could not sleep. Tomorrow would come too soon. I was trying to remember my biofeedback lessons, trying to find some peaceful moment to think about while I slowed my breathing, tried to shut my eyes. So I thought about two summers ago, when Jay and I were in Hawaii. We'd gone snorkeling every afternoon of the vacation. But I was always afraid to breathe underwater, afraid to look down and see the flickerings and shadows I imagined down there, afraid of the dorsal fin cutting through the water beyond the shallows. I'd panic and yank my head out of the water and swim straight back to shore every time.

We only had one good face mask, so we'd been taking turns. But on that last afternoon, Jay put on the old fins and swam out with me. He took my hand and guided me toward the coral beds, while I snorkeled along. Finally, I lifted my head out of the water and looked toward shore. We were far, far out beyond the point. I put my head back in the water and floated on the billowy drowse. No fear of sea snakes, or eels coiled between the rocks, or shadowy manta rays drifting over the sand. Now I looked down and saw thousands of fish, schools of fish, darting and flitting with the currents. We floated there in the late afternoon sun like sea creatures, fearless and full of grace.

It was an image to hold onto. In the thinning light of the coming winter, it was a good thing to have in reserve. It was the most perfect image I could imagine, and so I put myself back to sleep with it, lying in the king-sized bed that long, Texas night.

The next morning the lobby was full of ROTC checking out, and loading onto the buses parked out front. White hats everywhere, bobbing and weaving and stumbling out the double doors. Well, thank goodness for that, I thought, as I detoured around them and doubled back so I could take the elevator up to the mezzanine. Somewhere up here was the Wrangler Room, which was where I was headed for a panel on Frontier Myths. This morning I'd go to some panel sessions, take notes, learn something. Later this afternoon I'd give my paper.

I walked down the hall full of people like myself, wearing their conference badges, carrying their notebooks and pens, looking at their conference maps. I said hello to a few of them, hardly knew any by name. There was a funny smell in the air up here – like hair spray or perfume was being piped in through the air ducts. But there was the Wrangler Room. I was a little late, so I'd just slip in and sit in the back. I edged the door open and somebody grabbed my arm.

"The new concept is layering," the girl who had my arm was saying, as she began massaging my wrist with some kind of cream. She was wearing a white smock. So was everybody else in the room. "First you apply the primer, or the base, then the perfume, and then, the sealer." I tried to get my arm back.

"What is this?" I said, looking around. There were tables lined up against the walls. A kind of vapor hung over the room.

"It's the new line, hon. It's called 'Solitude.' Like it?"

I looked at my program again. Frontier Myths: Wrangler Room, Ten o'clock. Two men in tweed jackets pushed through the door. They took one look at that room and fled, like they'd just stumbled into the women's bathroom.

She looked at my conference badge. "So, Zoe, isn't this great?" She sniffed at my wrist. "I think it's fresher than 'Dimage.' Not as fruity, if you know what I mean." I just stood there. She looked at my badge again, and saw that it was just like hers, except mine said Western Literature Conference, and hers said, Western Cosmetology Conference. She dropped my hand.

"Oh. You're in the wrong room. That's happened all morning. Weird." She turned away and drifted back to the perfume display on the other side of the room. Four or five people came through the door, took one look and went right back out. What was I doing still standing here? I turned to go and just for an instant, saw someone out of the corner of my eye. "Who would you marry if you hadn't married Jay," my friend had asked that time at the beach. And there he was, the man himself, watching from the doorway, the very one I had named – the one who'd watched me out of the corner of his eye, as I had watched him, across the proverbial crowded room.

I looked at him standing there for just a moment, his head cocked to one side, his hand about to wave. I think he always waited upon an invitation, some signal or sign from me, but I had never given it, though I had wondered about it sometimes. I thought of that big, empty, bed in the hotel room, which would tell no secrets. It would be something to hold onto, some connection not threatened by CAT scans.

Ah, the widow surveys the empty bed. And who does she see? I looked at him standing there and knew now that I would never say his name. I knew what I had not known before. Standing in that room of scents and oils and potions, I knew for better or worse, I was going for broke now if it killed me. The widow surveys the empty bed, and what she sees is the empty bed. There wasn't anyone I could name, no name but Jay's. So I pretended I had not seen him, and turned back toward the woman in the white smock.

We learned later in the day that the hotel conference director had merged two computer programs and had somehow put the cosmetology exhibits in the rooms somebody else had assigned to the literature conference. But we eventually found our right rooms. My paper went all right, I guess. Given our slot at four thirty in the afternoon, it was a miracle anybody was there to hear it at all. As it was, there were only about half a dozen sleepy souls listening politely as the four of us on the panel ground our way through the end of the afternoon. Polite, weary applause at the end, then everybody got up and fled the room. Any questions from the audience? Not today, thank you. What was I doing here anyway? I went back up to my room, ordered room service and took a long hot bath. Maybe this was what I was doing here.

I could hear the phone ringing in the next room. What now? Well, I wouldn't run to the phone. That was no way to live. I slipped on my robe and walked to the bed, sat down, took a deep breath. It was Jay.

"I tried to get her to go outside this morning, but she wouldn't budge," he was saying, "so I picked her up and took her out back. But she just lay back down on the grass. She was still there this afternoon when we all got home, so I'll probably take her in in the morning." He slipped that in just as smoothly as you please, like he was taking her to the vet's for booster shots or nail clipping. "I just wanted you to know what's been going on around here." He said it so casually, so gently, I knew it would happen now.

"But I'll be home day after tomorrow," I said. I looked at the clock. Seven thirty. "I don't think she can wait that long."

"But I wanted to be there to see her out, you know?"

"I know, Zoe, but I don't think I can wait that long."

I was always the one who took her to the vet, I was the one she wouldn't look at all the way home. Jay'd never seen how she hated that place, how she always knew when we pulled into the parking lot, how she'd crouch down and refuse to get out of the car.

"Maybe I could get an emergency flight change or something."

"I doubt if you could do that for a dog."

"But I didn't want you to have to do this alone."

"I'll be okay."

"What'll you tell the kids?"

"The truth."

"Don't take them along, okay?"

"I wouldn't do that. They can say goodbye to her here."

I wanted to come home right then, but I was stuck there over a Saturday night with my no-changes, low-fare plane ticket.

"Well, at least this way I'll still get to see where Kennedy got shot."

Jay laughed. "That should be a real mood brightener." I'd signed up for the Saturday afternoon trip to the Texas School Book Depository Building that came along with the conference package

"I don't like being so far away," I said, then stopped myself. No point in going any further now. So I said goodbye to Jay and turned on the first Showtime movie I could find. I didn't care what it was.

The drive into Dallas from the hotel was a series of on and off ramps that circled back so many times I had to hold on tight to the seatback in front of me and concentrate on anything in the distance that stayed still. It was the way the whole trip had felt.

It had been a bitter joke I'd heard repeated all through this crazy conference: what a great way to end the whole thing – a field trip to where Oswald had pulled the trigger. But I was getting second thoughts about this, as I stepped off the bus into the thick, muggy air of downtown Dallas. My seatmate on the bus was having second thoughts too. In fact she'd decided she wouldn't even go in. She'd walk around outside, maybe look up at the window from the sidewalk.

The lobby was cool and dark, and just what you'd expect. I paid my five dollars for the headset and wandered over to the elevator to the sixth floor. It felt like a mausoleum – dark, chilly, air conditioning on too high. I supposed this was better than sitting around the hotel thinking about what Jay was doing today, but now I wasn't so sure.

The entire sixth floor of the building was a museum – and cold and dark like the lobby. I wished I'd brought a sweater. We put on our headsets and began to play the tape that would take us, hour by hour, through those four days in November, as we wandered through a maze of photographic murals.

I turned up the volume. I could hear the commentator announce the arrival of the plane at Love Field, could hear the crowd cheering and clapping in the background. Then there they were, the two of them, coming out of the plane into the morning sun. What did they know, waving to the crowd, their faces to the sun that bright day? What did they know, stepping into that open, waiting car with the top down, thank God the weather had cleared.

I turned a corner and came to a section of the exhibit with chairs lined up in front of a screen. So this was the part you needed to sit down for, I thought, as I made my way to a second row chair. We heard the motorcade, the cheering, the clapping, the commentator announcing the journey of that car down Main Street – past the jail, past the bank, then the old courthouse, now the grassy knoll of

Dealy Plaza up ahead. We held our breath. We knew what was coming. We leaned forward in our seats, put a hand out, but the motorcade kept on, there was no stopping it now. It turned off Main Street onto Houston, passing the intersection of Houston and Elm, then the sharp left turn toward the underpass in the distance, and looming over that funny zigzag in the road, an old warehouse, nothing to look at, with the Hertz sign sitting on top, telling the time.

The band-tailed pigeons sat on the rooftops in the sun, indifferent to the motorcade seconds from the cool, dark, quicksilver safety of the underpass. But what was that? A thousand birds rushed skyward, a thousand birds splintering the sky. Now what had frightened those birds? Then the sudden quiet and the birds gone from that faultless, waiting sky.

The man sitting in front of me put his arm around his wife, and they leaned together as tears ran down their faces. Everybody there with the exception of a couple of teenagers knew the rest by heart.

They just ran out of luck that day, though all along maybe they weren't so lucky as they seemed. Still, we thought they'd live forever. I walked over to the window where Oswald had stood that day, and looked out. Just an ordinary city street, framed on either side by that funny little park. If you were to stand there by that northeast window, seeing what he saw, you'd want to shout, "duck!" but of course nobody's listening, and nobody ducks. They're still sitting there with their smiling faces turned to the sun, about to wave at the little kid whose daddy has just hoisted him up on his shoulders, "Wave, sonny," he says, and so he does.

Weren't we always ready to believe in conspiracy? Didn't we want order even there in that appalling chaos? I thought of that dark, crazed gunman who'd managed to get all the luck that day. Even a conspiracy was preferable to that unreasoning, frenzied blip in the workings of the universe. Ah, we always wanted reasons good enough. I thought about Jay and how nobody'd ever given him a reason.

I looked up at that same hot, thin sunlight, that same perilous autumn sky. I saw the hand raised against the blow that had already fallen, saw her hand outstretched to pull him back before it was too late, but he was already gone. I thought of my father, in the hospital once already now, my mother at war with all the germs of the world, lining up the vitamins for the day on the kitchen breakfast table, like her own private arsenal – A through Z, plus some letters nobody'd ever heard of, her own secret elixir. She made him wear a hat and coat out to the sidewalk for the mail, read every book on nutrition she could find, wrapped him in such care I wondered if he were suffocating in this slow, quiet fadeout. It was all happening long distance now. I could barely imagine it. "Still working on the book?"

"Oh yes, making progress all the time, I'm almost done now," his voice on the phone as strong as ever.

Winter would be moving in soon. She'd have put on the flannel sheets by now, guarding against damp and chill and draft everywhere she could. She'd watch him asleep in his chair, the channel changer in his lap, his reading glasses sliding down his nose, she'd watch and say, "I don't think he's any paler than he was last fall. I'm sure he always slept in his chair like that." I had not resolved it, though, which way you'd want it, if you had the choice. Sad and slow, everyday a goodbye, or like a thunderbolt out of the sky, no time for goodbye at all. I'd never be like my mother, though. Yes I would. I already was.

I looked at my watch, and wondered what Jay was doing. I could see him sitting on the floor of the examining room, Niki's head on his lap while the vet gave her the injection. Jay was stroking her head, so she wouldn't mind the needle. How simple this was. How complicated.

I could hear everything turning breathless and still.

"She's gone now," the vet was saying. He touched Jay on the shoulder and cleared his throat.

Jay was getting up. "Good-bye, girl," he said, looking down at her one more time before he turned away for good. They'd let him out the back door. It wouldn't do anybody any good to have him walk through the waiting room looking like that. Why the white-haired woman with the basset hound would get up and head for the door just like she did a week ago. This time she'd change vets altogether.

The flight home was over in seconds. I sat there huddled against the window, looking out at the sky. I cried all the way home, turned toward that flawless blue sky.

My seatmate kept shooting me glances over his half-glasses. I could tell he was just pretending to read. My dark glasses and lap full of shredded Kleenex were a dead giveaway.

"A death in the family?" he finally asked.

"Oh, no," I said. "Just the dog."

We landed as the trip had begun – in a rainy mist.

But on the drive around the lake coming home, I could see the sun beginning to catch a little wave here and there, could see those gauzy clouds beginning to dissolve.

All the way home the kids kept exchanging secret glances. And lots of whispering and shushing I wasn't supposed to notice coming from the back seat. We drove up our little hill, and the first thing I saw watching out the picture window was the face that was not there. Then something silvery waving in the breeze caught my eye. I turned around as Jay pulled into the driveway. It was an old Happy Birthday banner wrapped around the top of a tiny evergreen somebody had stuck on that little hill the kids called Fernyland, where over the years we'd buried the bird, three or four gerbils, goldfish too many to count, a couple of lizards, an entire ant farm and one well-loved stuffed animal who had died in the washing machine.

The kids carried my suitcase and overnight bag into the house. I went into the living room and stood looking out the window. Now I could see there were streamers and ribbons over every piece of standing vegetation. We'd wanted to bury Niki at home, but as it turned out, medical science kept her. The kids wanted to have the funeral anyway, and this was it. I wondered if all this was real to them. But the kids were old hands at it. I, on the other hand, never was.

"I let everybody do exactly what they wanted to out there, so I'm not responsible," Jay said.

I laughed. It looked like Mardi Gras, or Christmas or maybe Halloween, it was hard to tell.

I put my arms around his waist, tucked my head under his chin. "It was great that you did all this," I said, looking over at the cake on the dining room table. It said, "Happy Birthday Irene." I looked again.

"Who's Irene?"

"I have no idea," Jay said.

"Dog cake?" I said.

"Of course."

"No dog," I said.

Jay just looked at me and plowed on ahead. "Anyway, the kids thought they might get the dogs from down the street to come up. Don't worry, we've got an ice cream cake in the freezer for us." We'd always celebrated dog birthdays by getting a leftover cake at the supermarket. That was part of the pleasure – finding the most disgusting cake in the store, then feeding it to the birthday dog and any other dogs that might be passing by.

I wondered about good old Irene, though, and why somebody'd ordered a birthday cake for her and then didn't pick it up. Maybe it was Irene herself. Maybe she changed her mind about having a birthday. I sat down at the dining room table and stared at that cake. Jay'd gone outside.

The voice on the answering machine had been whispery and tremulous. It was a couple of weeks ago when I'd been cleaning up old messages. This is Irene something or other, she was saying. She was trying to reach the surgeon who'd removed part of her colon a month ago because she was sure it had spread to her breasts, for when she woke up this morning her breasts were aching, or maybe it was her heart, she couldn't tell. I hate to bother you like this, but would you have just a minute to call me back? Ah, so apologetic, so polite. She'd need more fight than that, I wanted to tell her. Scream at that doctor for not calling you back even if you did reach the wrong number. Well, even I knew cancer didn't work that way. But here was this broken person who'd called my number by mistake. She'd probably been sitting in her rocker by the phone since yesterday, twisting the handkerchief in her lap, and patting her chest, and trying to take long, slow breaths, she couldn't bother him again, he was so busy, otherwise he'd have called her back she was sure, but oh my, she couldn't wait like this much longer.

I knew by that voice she'd wait days before trying him again. What was I, a conduit for pain these days? I seemed to gather it up like a human lodestone. In some perverse way didn't I beckon these sorrows? Well, I didn't want to call her back

"You called the wrong number," I said as gently as I could. "You called me by mistake. But look," I said, "I really don't think it spreads like that. I'm sure the doctor will tell you that. You should call him right back." So I wished her well, and erased her from the machine. Now here she was back again on this birthday cake for the dog funeral. Of course there were a million Irenes in the world. Still, I wondered about this one and why she never got her birthday cake. Well, it was fit for the dogs, now.

I looked at the cake again. Happy Birthday, Irene, I said, it's good to be home. Sitting there in the dining room with the late afternoon sun coming at last through the cathedral window, it was good to be home.

The kids kept running in and out of the house, carrying things. The sun was going down, and Jay told the kids it was now or never. Soon it would be too dark. So they called me outside and we gathered around the little tree with the silver birthday banner and said goodbye.

The kids were getting ready to bury an old metal chest they'd found in the garage. They'd collected Niki's things and laid them one by one in the bottom of the chest – her collar, her red leash, her dish with her name in big, gold, stick-on letters, Squeaker, her favorite chase toy, her half-chewed dog pepperoni stick.

Will began. "Everybody needs to say something funny about Niki."

Jillie raised her hand, according to the script they'd written. I could see her behind the scenes, battling to go first. She cleared her throat. "I remember that time Niki barfed on Daddy." Truth to tell it was the funniest thing any of us could remember, except for Jay, of course, who still didn't think it was very funny. I wondered what it would be like to have an eye-level view of such a thing. You didn't see canine projectile vomiting every day.

We'd all been in the bedroom saying goodnight to Jay, who was going to bed early so he could get up to go fishing in the morning. A friend was taking him out on the Sound. "Come here, girl," Jay said to Niki who was lying on the foot of the bed. "Come here." He was lying there propped up on the pillows, patting his chest. "Now who do you love best?" He winked at the kids. Niki got up and went over to him, and just stood there. "Give me a kiss."

"It splatted all over daddy's face, " Jillie said, "like it came out of a big hose."

Jay couldn't believe it. It had indeed splatted all over his face, his chest, and down his arms. "Oh, shit!" he said, jumping out of bed.

"Don't you mean barf?" I called after him, as he raced into the bathroom and into the shower. Niki watched him run down the hall, walked over to the edge of the bed and did it again.

"Wow!" Will said. He couldn't believe it either. "It went so far."

We stood there in the sun going down, trying to remember how funny it was, and how much we had all laughed. Nobody said anything. Then Max told about the time she climbed onto the roof from the back deck. We looked up from dinner and there she was, looking back at us through the window. And so it went.

The light was almost gone now. The trees near the edge of the gully rose up against the purple sky. We could see the moon coming up from behind the hill. "You guys better skip the long part," Jay said. "It's getting too dark to see." They were going to read some poems.

"I don't have to see. I know mine by heart," Jillie said.

"Go ahead," Will said. Then she read *Goodnight Moon* because it was her favorite book. She loved the old lady bunny who whispered hush as she sat rocking by the fire, who watched over the baby bunny in the big bed, and the kittens and the mittens and the mouse in the corner. That book always comforted her some way, and every night it settled her down to sleep.

"Goodnight kittens, Goodnight mittens
Goodnight nobody, Goodnight mush.
Goodnight to the old lady whispering hush."

And there was Irene herself, sitting in the rocking chair by the phone, by the moon coming in the window, by the kittens and the mittens, and the socks hung by the fire. Goodnight, Irene, I thought, the song is for you, it was always for you.

Jillie finished the story and laid the book in the chest. "Goodnight Niki whispering hush."

Jay flicked on his flashlight while the kids planted sunflower seeds, the biggest flower they could think of. I thought about spring and what the yard would look like with all those sunflower stalks pushing their way up, grinning and nodding their approval all summer long.

We came inside and had our ice cream cake instead of dinner. The house grew dark and quiet. Somebody needed to turn on a light, or the television or the radio. But the kids had all gone downstairs, where it was too quiet, too. I went into the living room and sat down on the floor by the coffee table. There was my overnight bag in the middle of the room. No need to worry about putting it away now. I picked up the picture of Jay and Niki hiking the Pacific Crest Trail. The sun was shining down on everything – the snow, the mountains in the distance, shining down on Niki, shining down on Jay.

I sat there for a long time, listening to the quiet. No toenails skidding around the corner, no tail thumping against the wall, or chink of her collar, or the sound of her yawn, or her sigh as she settled into sleep. What was sorrow anyway, but this? The sound of absence everywhere.

The Year of the Tent Caterpillar

Beverly Conner

She'd never even had to think about it before. He'd always been there in the spring – pruning, weeding, fertilizing, spraying, and whatever else a man does in the garden. She hadn't really paid that much attention to the details, knowing that he was near. It was their major division of labor. Luke nurtured the garden – lawn, trees, vegetables, shrubs, a few flowers – while she created lemon mousse, spinach (his) salad, and quiche Lorraine. She could bone a chicken breast in seconds, and her crème brulee melted even the hard-core dieter.

With two jobs between them – she taught Economics at the university and he taught high school math – they split the other chores down the middle. Luke cleaned the bathrooms of their small two-storied Cape Cod house because Aline never could understand how a civilized person could stick her hand down a toilet, but she dusted because he could not bear the tedium of static knickknacks.

And so it went, though frequently they flowed into

one another's area, as when she sprouted radish and alfalfa seeds, turning the damp sprouts twice each day in a big glass jar whose mouth she'd covered with a rubber-banded square of pantyhose. Luke called it her drainboard garden, but it was he who thought to sprinkle the sprouts on top of her cheese and anchovy crostini – hot, buttery hors d'oeuvres they served with a white Italian Chianti – and later to bake them into the whole wheat bread she kneaded each Saturday morning.

But that, she reminded herself for the hundredth time, was last spring. She supposed it was one of the interminable phases of bereavement (a word cold and waxy like calla lilies), but for weeks she had begun these warm reminiscences from their nine years together only to end in fury that he could have left her so swiftly and with such silence.

"Expired at approximately 3:30 A.M." That was supposed to describe what had happened as they lay sleeping with the covers thrown back that warm night last July. Expired – as if his essence had sighed and slipped out the window open to the scent of three hawthorn trees that bordered the yard. Anger gnawed at her when she remembered finding him that morning lying on his back, his arms akimbo beneath his head, ankles crossed. It was a damned jaunty position in which to die. She had recently read that sleep positions describe personalities; those who sleep as she found Luke tend to control their environments (the rows of Bibb lettuce and zucchini and Jerusalem artichokes). Where, she wondered, was his control when he became a tanned, forty-one-year-old cardiovascular accident? Where was his sense of symmetry when a clot lodged in his left coronary artery, and he joined the hundreds of thousands each year whose first symptom of myocardial infarction is death? Oh, she had learned a great deal about heart attacks these past ten months.

But lately the fury had subsided to irritation, which somehow seemed even less worthy than the anger. She supposed it signaled the beginning of a new phase. Aline's eyes were bitter as she mentally ticked off the Seven Aspects of Bereavement, right out of the Widows' Counseling Service brochure: fear, helplessness, inadequacy, vulnerability, anger, and that never-ending, over-riding ache of loneliness. And don't forget guilt – because you're alive and he's not... he's not....

She sat in the May twilight, looking at the hawthorn trees from the bedroom window. Why had he never told her about them? She shivered: hundreds of thousands of crawling creatures no more than a fraction-of-an-inch long, constantly in motion, writhing within the sheer, white cocoons out of which they'd spawned, the tips of the hawthorn branches covered with the sticky, spun-gauze halos. They dripped through the webs off the trees so that she no longer stepped barefooted (or any other way) across Luke's fine-bladed Kentucky bluegrass. She'd never even seen a bug on those trees before. Had he sprayed late each fall or early each spring? Had she been negligent, or was it simply as the Sunday supplement of the Tacoma paper proclaimed, "The Year of the Tent Caterpillar"?

She knew she could ask for help. Several of their friends (she still thought in plural pronouns) – even Mr. Thornton up the street – would spray the trees or do whatever was necessary. She could easily phone a gardening service or an exterminator. There were alternatives; she'd coped with home maintenance all winter, and long before that. Luke hated making repairs, and though he could prune the Christmas holly from their twenty-foot tree without a scratch and not even wear gloves, hand him a hammer and he began quietly to curse the "perversity of inanimate objects."

Maybe that was her problem. The caterpillars were not inanimate. They were voracious and advancing, an invasion stripping the hawthorn of its beauty and rapaciously devouring its life.

My god, she thought, they are, after all only bugs. She must be even more depressed than she realized to see a garden chore, though admittedly hard and unpleasant, as an invasion. She prickled with embarrassment at her descent into melodrama. Just insects. But her appetite was ruined, and she put the loin lamb chop she had thawed for her dinner back into the refrigerator for another night.

Driving home from the nursery the next morning, Aline watched for hawthorns. They were a popular tree in the Northwest, and she saw that many bore the tented cocoons and ravishment of the caterpillars, the delicate leaves and bright pink blossoms masticated to crusty brown. The woman at Carini's nursery had been very helpful, showing her how to screw the nozzle of the hose onto the jar of insecticide, the water automatically diluting the concentrate and dispensing a deadly mist as high as the top of the fifteen-foot trees. In fact, the caterpillars were such a problem this year that the nursery provided Xeroxed instructions. Aline shook her head: not only was she going to spray them, but she'd taken the morning off work, canceling a class, as if the trees might somehow be consumed (she didn't say dead) before Saturday. She hadn't missed a day since Luke's funeral.

Twenty minutes later, she was reaching into the back of her closet for her paint-stained jeans. A smear of pale gold across one pocket flung her back two years into the night they'd painted the bedroom, Luke sliding the roller like golden rays of morning sun across the faded blue walls. They'd drunk hot coffee from a thermos and finally switched toward dawn to the tall bottles of German beer that Luke liked so much.

Aline gripped the jeans and roughly pulled them on along with Luke's ancient Mariners cap, a pun he always chuckled over. She ran down the stairs and out to the storage shed in the back yard, grabbed everything the list said she would need, and carried it out to the front where she'd left the insecticide.

Aline uncoiled the hose, dragged it near the hawthorns, and attached the jar of pale liquid. Its black and yellow letters read Spray-N-Slay. She turned on the water full force, then approached the sprayer cautiously. Holding it straight-armed in front of her, she aimed it at the trees, took a few steps forward, and pressed the release nozzle. Like a colorless flame-thrower, the deadly spray hit the nearest tree in a shower of crystal needles. The morning was still, and the spray moved exactly as Aline directed it with no drift. Gradually calming, she realized that it was hardly different from watering the lawn, the sound of it as gentle as rain, and when she could bend her attention from the barely discernible movement within the sheer tents, the spray seemed a quiet beneficence.

Methodically she sprayed each of the three trees, stepping no closer than was necessary, until the jar was emptied. She turned off the water and quickly picked up the long-handled tree pruner. With a sharp breath she moved to the first tree. At the nursery they'd suggested one procedure or the other, but Aline wasn't taking any chances.

The cocoons looked like bandaged appendages spiking out from all sides. Very carefully, she extended the pruning shears upward until they bit into a dripping branch. She stood as far to one side as possible to be out of the way when it dropped, and one by one the white-thumbed limbs cracked to the ground.

Panting, she moved to the second tree. Her arms ached from the awkward and unfamiliar work. On the final tree, she noticed that her face felt wet. She wiped her cheek against one shoulder, and the sleeve came away charcoal-smudged with mascara. She hadn't known she was crying.

Stepping among the corpse-like branches, her stomach taut with revulsion, she held her breath to make sure any movement might not be hers and studied the cocoons intently. Most of the caterpillars were dead.

Aline picked up the light aluminum snow shovel Luke had used no more than half-a-dozen times during their mild winters. It was like a giant spatula, wider than long, and with it she carried two or three branches at a time over to the center of the concrete driveway. Her blouse was damp from the exertion, and she used the back of her hand to wipe her forehead, wondering how many times she'd have to wash before she could believe her fingers were free of the last trace of poison.

When the infested branches were piled in the driveway, Aline picked up the can of charcoal lighter fluid. She dumped the entire contents on the heap of limbs, letting it gurgle out as she held the can limply. Tossing it back onto the lawn, she took a book of matches from her jeans pocket. She struck and lit each match, not even stooping but just tossing them lighted onto the wood. The fluid ignited immediately, and grudgingly the wood, green and wet from late spring rains, began to burn. The cocoons shriveled as fast as the flames tongued them, and Aline stepped back from the heat, knowing all the caterpillars weren't dead, and what a rotten way to celebrate the Rites of Spring, anyway. She didn't want to think about the living ones, yet that was the whole purpose of the fire, to destroy the tent caterpillars once and for all in the flames.

And surely the crackling and hissing was only wet wood, and pray god she wouldn't hear a scream, thin and tiny, and she knew her reaction was extravagant because everyone burned garden refuse in this part of the county, and it wasn't Luke blazing in a circle no more than five feet across (why even think it?), not big enough to be a man, nor children burning (Lady Bug, Lady Bug, fly away home —), but only insects, thousands of voracious, crawling caterpillars heaped on a funeral pyre.

And she didn't hear a scream, not even her own which she swallowed before it could fly out. Her panic subsided as the flames died to a few quietly burning branches, innocent-looking as a fire for roasting marshmallows. The caterpillars were gone... expired... suspired... and she leaned wearily on the handle of the snow shovel. Aline looked at the hawthorn trees. They were free and clean, and the remaining dark pink buds glowed in the morning sun. Though ragged from her inexperienced pruning, they would make it through the spring.

The Green Bird

Hans Ostrom

My appointment with the psychologist, Roberta, is at 5:00 p.m. It takes about ten minutes to walk there, but I decide to leave the house at 4:17 and take a circuitous route. Vigorous exercise helps mental health, says Roberta.

Tacoma in November: dark, cold, wet. You notice the trees – laurels and firs, especially. They seem so heavy in November. They engulf houses. Are not just evergreen but ever-growing – relentlessly green. They grab evening light greedily. They soak up rain, mist, and fog. You walk by them, breathing vigorously, and they seem to know exactly what to do with your white clouds of carbon monoxide. Last week I tried to tell Roberta this. I thought it would be a light, ironic way to begin the session: "knowledgeable tree waits for vigorous walker to pass by." But Roberta wasn't having any of it.

"What are you really trying to say, Nancy?" she asked.

I had gone into the session feeling pretty good, but she brought me right down with that one. What *was* I really saying? Christ, who can answer that? I was really saying that I hated to wear skirts in November. I was really saying that traversing Tacoma in evening is like walking in a cave. I was really saying that one of my favorite meals is sautéed shrimp dolloped on steamed rice. What *was* I really saying, Roberta? You tell me. Jesus, sometimes I wish I'd chosen the only man in the clinic. Maybe he would have smiled and said, "I've often thought the same thing about evergreens." Is it so tough just to agree with somebody? Or to nod and move on to another topic? I mean, what if it turns out that what I was really saying was what I'd said? I have a lot of anger, as Roberta would say.

Anyway. I head up Fifth Street and then down Yakima Avenue. Glorious Yakima. It is populated with aristocratic trees. Venerable maples, stately elms. Now they are bare, like giants stripped to the waist. Pale streetlights give their branches a ghostly aspect.

The cars rip by, too fast as usual. Drivers and passengers are angry, hungry, late or discouraged. Or all four at once. At each street corner I pause like a foreigner, glancing four ways, not just two, crossing the street only when I can guarantee safety. "What does that say about you, Nancy?" The trouble with going to a therapist is that her voice perches on your shoulder like a squawky parrot – a bright green questioning bird waiting in the trees of November.

Let's stay on task. I promise to move us down Yakima: here we go. We are almost to Sixth Avenue. We've reached a huge old brick apartment house. We look up, and we see a bald man in a white sweater fiddling clumsily with his blinds. We see yellow, cracked paint on his ceiling. We imagine the rest: a tea kettle steaming in a cramped kitchen; a small television murmuring; a cat sleeping; magazines we would never read lying on a chipped coffee table; clipped, expired coupons in a drawer.

We're on the move. We see the bright Shell station, lit up in the gloom. Cars on the rack, cars already fixed, cars at the pumps. Customers feeding their credit cards, mere morsels, to petroleum-dispensers.

We – oh, never mind: I know you're not really with me. I decide on a whim to go into Wasserstrom's Flower Shop. It has vases and pots in a display window and a jungle of flowers and plants between me and Mrs. Wasserstrom, crouched at her cash register, reading *T.V. Guide*. How rare it is to see someone still reading *T.V. Guide*. Again there is dandruff on her navy blue polyester blazer.

"Yes! Can I help you?"

"Yes! Do you have mixed bouquets?"

Because Mrs. Wasserstrom speaks breathlessly, I feel as though I should respond in kind.

"Well, yes! We have some and we can make some up. We can mix carnations and baby's breath with a few roses, for example, or daisies and carnations and a few other things, and we start at" – she recites the prices – "but they're very special, and we can make up almost anything you like."

I name the price I deem as fine.

"There's a card over there," she says. She has ceased speaking breathlessly.

I write on a card for my co-worker Dennis Campion, who is leaving the firm to go back to Australia.

We'll miss you, I write with the grimy pen on a small pink card with a dash of flowers in the corner. I am surprised the card reminds me of those things they hand out at funerals. All pre-printed except for the name of Our Dearly Departed. Then I write, *I'll miss you. Good luck! Nance*. I watch the ink in my name go from wet and gleaming to absorbed and flat. Then I seal the envelope and give it to Mrs. Wasserstrom. I hear myself sounding efficient.

"If you could deliver it on Thursday."

"Oh, yes, I'll write *Thursday* down here, and I'll make it a very *nice* mixed bouquet for your friend" – she reads the card –" your friend Mr. Campion."

"All right," I say, finishing the check, not wanting to use a credit card, not carrying enough cash. "Is today the nineteenth?"

"Oh yes! The nineteenth!"

Mrs. Wasserstrom: still energetic, full of verve at nearly five for flowers and plants and customers and billing and salesmanship – old-fashioned salesmanship, breathless when it needs to be.

Out the door I go, with a loud ring I hadn't noticed going in, wool cap reapplied to head. Oddly, I don't recall having removed the cap. I cut down Third instead of going all the way to Sixth Avenue. This is my first mistake.

I walk past the Lutheran Outreach Services building, and see, appended to the sign, a smaller sign that says, "Mental Health Services Upstairs." I look up at the only lighted window and there is the head of Kathy Hauser, a co-worker. Her head is talking grimly to an unseen counselor. Sturdy Kathy needs counseling, too? Of course she does. Who doesn't? Nonetheless, sight of her throws me off.

I make my second mistake. I allow myself, there in the

dark and the cold, to have a mild anxiety attack. A brief turn of the stomach, an *ad hoc* gathering of perspiration at the small of the back, a sprinting of the pulse, a sense of being overwhelmed.

My third mistake is to decide to smoke a cigarette to counteract the anxiety. I turn my back on the Lutheran Outreach Services building, bring out a pack of Kools and light up, taking menthol down to my toes.

It helps. I watch the traffic, listen to water hiss under radial tires, pay attention to Tacoma as its hungry, angry, discouraged, tired citizens go home or go to the swing shift.

My fourth mistake is to calm down. Kathy Hauser fairly ambushes me. Suddenly she's on the street and coming around in front of me.

"Nancy! I thought it was you."

She looks – well, drawn. She has that run-through-the-mill look I must have after a visit with Roberta.

"What are you doing here?" she asks.

"Oh – out for a walk. Good for the heart, you know." Then of course I make a joke about the cigarette. It hits Kathy all wrong. Her mood becomes severe.

"Nancy, I – I hope you won't tell anyone about – about my counseling."

"Counseling?"

"Come on, Nancy, let's not be cute. You see the sign and the only light on." I want to tell her everyone goes to counseling now, except the ones who need it most, but I can see she harbors old-fashioned shame. Having to talk to a therapist makes her feel weak.

I also recognize in her, however, the over-aggressiveness that a fresh tussle with a counselor will induce, and

I find it cute, even though Kathy tends to be aggressive anyway, and even though she has directed both of us not to be cute.

"Now, why would I tell anybody? What's to tell? It's your affair."

"I'm sorry. You're right. Some people think you're nuts if you even think about going to a counselor, let alone go."

"Some people are wrong. Don't worry about it. I won't tell a soul."

"All right. See you at work. Enjoy your walk."

My walk. She leaves me to ponder my little white lie of omission – not mentioning my own appointment.

My cigarette would die a quick natural death on the wet sidewalk, but I crush it out anyway, and then go on my way, ostensibly to the session. It is 4:37.

I don't want to make a fifth mistake, but I do want to stop by the Carmen Brothers' grocery, which lies between me and Roberta's office. The practical reason is that I am down to four Kools, forlorn in a crumpled pack. But more, the Carmens' grocery is a fine place on dark Northwest evenings because the older folks in the neighborhood stop in then. They are immensely patient and infinitely interested in what they buy. They have time for life again, unlike the rest of us. They can stand for a full fifteen minutes in front of the cheese, never-minding other shoppers or the passage of time, to which they've already surrendered. They go slowly. They mistrust their carts. They study lists. Bless them, is what I say. It is a neighborhood amenable to older folks, and they reward the neighborhood with their persistence, with all the years they have lived, with all the things they are now able to ignore, with a certain slant of light in their faces and eyes.

Inside, I see one of the checkers greet a customer, a slender white-haired woman whose glasses have fogged.

"Mrs. Duffy," the checker says. "Let me wipe your glasses." And the checker takes the glasses from the woman and polishes them with her handkerchief; meanwhile, Mrs. Duffy's face looks somewhat embarrassed, revealed. But Mrs. Duffy is waiting.

"Thank you. Thank you, dear. Now I can see."

"You have your list?" asks the checker.

"I have my list."

She has her list. She chooses her cart.

Mistake Number Five – yes, yes, I know: I count compulsively – occurs when, once back outside, I don't stride boldly toward Roberta's. I linger in front of the grocery store: cars going by, shoppers going in, coming out, the invisible Northwest sky raining. Everyone in the city, it seems, is not in the proper place, is needing to be somewhere else. Fast. I force myself to recall the man I saw in the window. I imagine his being where he needs to be already. His home may not be much, but at least he is at it, I tell myself.

When I do start walking, I find myself at the corner of Tacoma Avenue, and you don't have to know Tacoma to know that I have a choice there. I choose *left* over *Roberta*.

"Not tonight, green bird," I say to the fowl that's glided down from a limb and alighted on my shoulder.

"Squawk!" I can hear Roberta saying as she scribbles *No Show* on my card or in her computer. "Squawk! What are you really saying?!" I imagine her sighing and being relieved that, according to the rules, she may bill me for the visit without having had to listen to me. I don't take it personally. I make sure my cell-phone is off because I don't want it to vibrate when Roberta or her receptionist calls. Not answering it is not enough. It must be off.

I light a Kool, hunch my shoulders, and head up the hill, up Tacoma Avenue toward home. Near the top of the hill, I see a terribly round man – the novels would say *portly* – in a thick wool coat, with a wool hat on his white head and water glistening on his red, jowly face. He is wheezing from his car up some steep steps to his house. His wife, with nothing on her head, greets him halfway up, takes his briefcase and says:

"Come inside. It's awful out here."

When I reach home, I let the cat in. Guilt hugs me like a husband I no longer love. I toss my coat on a chair and give the guilt a peck on the cheek. *Hi, Guilt! I'm home!* I turn the thermostat up and hear the furnace grumble in the basement.

It is 5:07. I am officially, blessedly late. What I have done is walk myself away from Roberta. I have walked past knowledgeable trees with green birds in them, and I have pieced together a dream of Tacoma, in which a friend's troubled head appears in a window, in which an overworked checker pauses to polish a pair of fogged glasses and a woman without a coat or a hat helps her husband up concrete steps he used to take two at a time, in which a woman mystified by her own efficiency writes a check for a mixed bouquet.

At 5:17 mischievous spirits unravel the cat, and she leaps in the air, twisting her spine and YEOWing at the apex of the jump. Then she shakes her fur and, with perfect posture, walks back to the kitchen.

At 5:23 I sit down with a glass of red wine to take inventory. First I read on the front page of the newspaper that last night a man walked to a gas station, pumped 94 gallons of fuel onto the pavement around him, sat down, lit a match, and burned himself up. I put the newspaper down. I don't wonder how they knew it was 94 gallons, but I do wonder why they reported it. I wonder when the shrinking newspaper will finally become a mere broadside, then disappear altogether. It is Merlot I'm drinking, I realize.

"Mrs. Wasserstrom," I say out loud. "And Kathy Hauser the Sturdy. And Dennis Campion, whom I will not see – ever – again, whom I could have fallen in love with, easily. And Mrs. Duffy and the checker, and the man with the red face and his wife and the man at his window fumbling with grimy blinds. And the people in the cars and on the street. And the customers and the mechanics." I really am talking out loud, but not loud. I am listening to the sound of my own voice.

By this time the cat is back in the living room and listening.

"Margo," I say to her, "you and I need to get to an airport or a train station. Fast. What am I really saying, Margo?" I ask. She plops down, purring. I am really saying that I've invited her on my lap, is what Margo thinks I'm saying.

I watch myself get up, sipping wine, and walk to the kitchen to prepare a modest meal and to mull over the ways in which I might speak to Roberta when next I see her. I could be contrite, or I could be cold, or I could have a lot of anger. And it all depends, I know, on what I think the green bird really wants to hear.

The Divination

Ann Putnam

It was just the two of us now, making our way through the late afternoon streets of Central Havana. Under this heavy, gauzy sky everything took on a bleached, dry feeling. It had the close, musty smell of unremembered rain. Some late afternoon high cloudiness had drifted in from the sea and tamped everything down into a sleepy, unguarded dream. I was glad we were going to the mountains tomorrow. I could hardly breathe.

Maria was watching the house numbers closely now. She said an address is hard to find here. She must find one doorway out of a hundred doorways. To me every street and cross street looked the same. If she disappeared I would be lost forever. There was no architectural extravagance here, not like Old Havana, where even the worst of the ruins held however precariously to a proud, Old World elegance. Here, the apartments jutted edge on edge into repeated rows of narrow doorways and dark, forbidding alleys. And only now and then the surprise of coming suddenly to a shirtless old man with slow and watchful eyes sitting on the doorstep, elbows on his knees, or an old woman in a faded blue dress standing against the door jamb, following us with her cautionary, narrowing gaze, a white bell of warning – *prohibido el paso*!

"You need to know that I will be translating, okay? I'll hear everything you say. What the *babalawo* says also. You will say important things without knowing it, and I will hear them."

I nodded. It was all right.

"You know how much it will be different from what you think? It's like this. In Cuba everything is always changing. By day everything is one thing and by night it's another. By day it's Santa Barbara but at midnight, you know, it's *Chango*. Nothing is simple like it looks. You know what I'm saying?"

When she'd said do you want to meet the *babalawo*, I had said please, yes, let's go there, why not? I was edging toward something that had beckoned to me in Old Havana. I had given something over to it but did not know enough to be afraid.

"Do you understand?" she said again. "The minute you set foot in his house you will see the night things. But it's secret and we must be careful. There can be danger."

My fortune told, my palm or tea leaves or Tarot cards read, it didn't matter; just no chicken blood. Only a cleansing, a healing of wounds, as Maria had promised. Only sweet and soft and nothing to fear. But I knew that whatever it was, I was going toward it now.

"I have to make a phone call," Maria said suddenly, pointing to the phone booth across the street. "Stay here and wait for me." She went to cross the street then turned back. "I know this looks like cops and robbers. But I am being very careful with you. Some *babalawos* are dangerous. Some of them are spies of the government. Who knows more secrets than they do? They can use your secrets against you. Some *babalawos* do terrible things. Sometimes they kill people." She could not alter the seriousness that rushed over her or leaven it with irony. She was no tour guide now and I was no tourist. What had started with the *santera* in Old Havana had led me here.

The streets seemed empty of everything but the heaviness of eyes. Behind doorways and half-shuttered windows, from narrow, dark alleyways, and here and there, cool and appraising glances floating down the street. And now the gaze of a woman in a yellow turban and gold earrings as I stood there, so obviously an intruder, my foreignness as weighty upon me as the humidity. I could feel my heartbeat in my hands, a rush of air down my throat.

I looked up at the sun coming slowly now through the thin layer of clouds as everything turned in slow motion. Maria came back over and took my hand. "A man in a red shirt will meet us on the corner," she said. "It's okay. Everything's okay now." She managed a half-smile but kept watch on the street ahead.

There were people everywhere now, making their way down this street or that, toward or away from the amazement of their everyday lives. We stood on the corner for five or ten minutes. She never took her eyes off the street ahead. She never let go of my hand.

Then there he was, making his way down the street toward us, his maroon shirt red enough for her to be absolutely sure now. We crossed the street to meet him and he kissed her on the cheek and shook my hand. There was a short, staccato exchange and then he turned and we followed him quickly, silently, block after block toward a distant salsa beat snapping with the pulse of the heat.

The haze was almost gone now. Any minute the sun would completely take the sky again. The man in the maroon shirt had gone on ahead. He'd stopped in front of a window with a yellow curtain billowing in the little breeze that had come up against the wrought iron grating. The man turned back toward the doorway where he stood for a moment without saying anything, then rang the bell. Maria squeezed my hand. I could feel her breath warm on my neck. It was clear even to me that something was about to change and that all three of us were waiting upon it.

The *babalawo* spoke only Spanish. What he said, he said to me, not to Maria, though I understood none of it. I thought of my dangerous American otherness and wondered if it was in some way a sin to be here. But I was here not as an anthropologist or scholar or tourist but as one of a thousand lost souls come in from the street.

He was a lovely looking, sixty-five year old man. He had a carefully trimmed white beard and close-cropped white hair under a gold crown. He was wearing a Baltimore Orioles baseball jersey, tie-dyed parachute pants and sports shoes. A hip high priest with a syncretism all his own. And around his neck a gold cross on a chain, yellow and amber beads for the goddess *Oshun*, and a string of white beads I could not identify.

The *babalawo* stretched out his legs and crossed his ankles and picked up his sacred book. It was full of numbers and markings and looked to be very old. He turned the pages carefully, then set it down. "He wants to know if you are ready," Maria said. "He has prayed to the dead of your family and to the *orishas* for permission of your guardian angel to conduct the divination."

"Tell him yes," I said. I unclenched my hands, unfurled my heart. Now he would tell me whose child I was, and what my future held.

Then he touched my forehead with his *opele*, the iron chain with the eight, two-sided coconut husks and threw it on the mat. He studied the pattern they made – which landed up and which landed down, like heads or tails, and in which order – and wrote down the pattern in his little book. Then he threw the chain again.

I was watching those dark, slender hands in a choreography of divination, and the way the chain and medallions flew across the mat. Finally his hand swept over the chain of coconut husks lying in a pattern only he could read, and he looked up at me and smiled. Then he said in English, "Laura. Daughter of *Oshun*," and he touched me on the forehead. Then he returned to the Spanish while Maria translated.

"Do you have family then?" the *babalawo* asked.

"A father," I said

"No husband or lover? No children?"

"No," I said.

"Are you menstruating?"

I turned to Maria. What did he mean?

"If you are menstruating," she said, "certain things have to be done differently."

"I'm not anymore," I said. How would I explain it?

"I've had, you know, a hysterectomy."

Maria's eyes widened. "Okay. No problem." She explained to him by cupping her hands below her waist and lifting them up.

"Ah," the *babalawo* nodded. So there would be no children to wish for. I touched my stomach.

Then he handed me a seashell and a bone. Bone of what, my eyes asked.

"It's all right," Maria said. "It's only goat vertebra." I closed my hand around it and shut my eyes. It felt strange and light in my hand. Then I slipped the seashell into my left hand, the bone into my right, and held out my hands.

He threw the *opele* again and pointed to the hand with the bone. Then he consulted his book and wrote down the *oddu*, the pattern and its legend. He threw it again. It came up seashell, then bone, then bone again and again and again. I did not take my eyes off his hands. Even from here I could see the pattern of 1's and 0's he was making, one under the other, until they made four lines across. Upside down they were hieroglyphs – marks and zeroes. My life.

Finally I looked over at Maria. Her face had undergone a transformation. It had clouded over completely. Her mouth was clamped tight. She was holding onto the edge of her chair.

"What's happening?" I whispered.

"The bone is very bad. There is very bad luck in the bone. He is finding out how it comes to you and what can be done to remove it."

But the *babalawo's* face did not change. The whole time the expression of transcendence and calm never left his face.

"Now he is asking what offerings must be made. Also what sacrifice."

I looked up at the crucifix that hung above him – the head hanging to one side, the bloody knees, the word *INRI* above the cross beam.

"Why do you come here?" the *babalawo* said. "What is the weight to be lifted?"

A fist of panic caught in my throat. What was there to say?

"What do you want?" he asked again.

What did I want? I wanted my shattered self knit back together. I wanted to be whole. "I don't want to be alone," I said. Tears that came from nowhere ran down my face.

"Do you wish for love then? Do you wish for someone to love you?"

"Oh, I don't know," I said. "I don't know about that." I looked at Maria.

"I know, she said. "Love is complicated."

"Yes," I said, "I'm afraid to wish for love."

"You should," she said. "You should always wish for it."

"All right," I said.

The *babalawo* nodded and smiled. "My child, my child," he said. Then he shut his eyes and began chanting in low, rich waves of sound.

All these years I had tried to beat back death with such an urgent eroticism, all I knew was the furious and unyielding insistence of my desire upon the moment. I had come unmoored, casting as I did filament after filament of myself into open air, then suddenly and always flung back to earth, and the loneliness afterward, a cold, old moon against a bleak, winter sky, a universe bereft of stars and human exhalation.

I had never been able to yield to the slow, more certain knowledge of heart touching heart, desire playing softly against my closed eyes, against my mouth, the sweet plum of faith on my tongue, the perfect supplicant.

I looked up at the statue of Christ on the wall and thought of everyone I knew who had been broken on the great, spiny wheel of life. I had been afraid of death my whole life. What I wanted was not to be afraid. What were those letters? What was *INRI*?

"You know," Maria said. "It's what Pontius Pilate said. Here he is. Jesus of Nazareth, King of the Jews. *I* for Jesus, *N* for Nazareth, *R* for King, *I* for Jews. You must not be Catholic," she said, smiling.

"No" I said, "I'm not anything." *INRI*. My body broken for you. *INRI*. Jesus. King of the Jews. The syncretism was so clear, yet so complicated.

The *babalawo* lay down the *opele* and looked at me. "There is a river to cross," he said. "Your heart is a strange darkness. Why is joy on the other side of the river?"

"So much loss," I said. "People who have died for no reason."

"Who? Who has died?"

It was all right. His eyes held me. Now I could say it. "My mother," I said. "And once a little baby girl. A long time ago. There has been an accumulation of sorrows." I looked at Maria. Her eyes were hot and dark.

"Fear or joy," the *babalawo* said. "One or the other."

Then he said, "Now you must hear a hard thing. Inside

your sorrow is a great anger you have never spoken. You are angry for things that could not be helped. You have anger for your mother and father for not safekeeping you."

There it was, all right, unclaimed all these years. "I know," I said. "My anger holds them to me. My anger fills the empty space of them. It keeps me safe."

"But anger takes up too much room. I will prepare an offering to take it away and replace it with a brand new thing. Three times a blessing will come to you."

I shut my eyes and shook my head.

Then the wife came back and motioned for us to follow her into the alley. "*Oshun* asks for a sacrifice," Maria said, "so she can help you."

"All right," I said, and I stepped into the narrow strip of light filtering down from the long thin rectangle of sky between the buildings.

Then there it was, just as I knew it would be, out of the corner of my eye, when I stepped into the alleyway. The dark shape tucked under the shadows – the thin, black-speckled hen in the cage by the wall. I thought of all the plump, white chickens on kitchen towels and pot holders and hot plates and little rugs in front of the stove. Chickens and cows. Eggs and milk. Red strawberries on blue and white checkered table cloths, the fat white chicken in the middle, picnics, birthdays, Fourth of July, all safe, all safe. How far this alleyway, how far that life.

The *babalawo* did not look up as we came and stood beside him, but continued making marks on the ground with a piece of white chalk – a smooth half circle in front of the altar and five or six crosses through the curve. Then he stood up and said a prayer to the sky, then a prayer to the altar he had made – a tureen with dark stones, another full of a dark-green liquid that caught the light, a vase with white and yellow flowers, a small, white candle, burning.

What do I remember of what happened next? Who can say why some things collect in the net of memory and other things fall through?

It squawked only once, struggling only a little at the beginning, when it was first lifted up. That wild little heart against his smooth, dark palms, the panicked flutter of wings. But then as he stroked it the hen became still. Only its eyes told it was alive. It did not flap its wings or cry out. Its own tiny self a willing sacrifice, its heart a slow and steady pulse. How do they live, these birds bound to earth as they are, what sense do they have of sky or sun, or flight?

The hen was offered to the tureen filled with that dark, glistening liquid. Would I have to drink it? I would be glad not to drink it. All right. I would do anything now. I had come to the dark center of otherness. It was as far as I had ever gone. I was being drawn toward things so far outside myself. I was in a country with no words I had ever known. I leaned over to take everything in. I would not shut my eyes, I would not miss a thing.

Then with the chicken in his hands, the *babalawo* made the sign of the cross – high up to the sky, down to the tureen with the stones, and then crossed himself, left then right, across his chest. "It is blood that is needed," the *bababalwo* said. "A sacrifice for *Oshun*. So she will help you." In that tight alleyway, the sun was edging its way down the high, grey walls.

Then the *babalawo* bent over and picked up the knife.

"Lamb of God, who takes away the sins of the world, hear our prayer."

He stroked the neck of the hen with the knife, and dark feathers drifted down through the light onto the offering. "Lamb of God, who takes away the sins of the world, have mercy on us."

Still, the hen lay quiet in his hands, the blinking eye the only sign of life, as the black feathers floated down through the holy light.

"Lamb of God, who takes away the sins of the world, grant us peace." He took up the chant again, this time low and sweet and soft, an incantation of love and death. Then he took the knife, and in a single, fluid gesture severed the artery.

The droplets glistened like little rubies in the light, over the offering for *Oshun*. Fruit and pumpkin seeds and purple flowers sprinkled with sugar and honey, all of it carefully placed on a square of brown wrapping paper, and now darkening brilliantly with blood. Then the *babalawo* lay the chicken on the pavement. I looked at it lying on the dark-stained concrete before the offering, a jumble of dark, scattered feathers.

Behind me were the spade and shovel. Gardening tools but there was no garden. Burial tools for graves of small significance.

"Was it a worthy offering?" he asked *Oshun*. Was I a worthy daughter? He dipped his hand in the dark liquid and shook it over the offering and sprinkled it on me. Then he nodded at me and smiled. Yes. It is a fine offering. All that is needed. So this was the necessary sacrifice. In death it seemed such a slight offering. The least of these, this small, diminished life, transfigured now through the awful blood. I looked at it lying there and felt the sun pouring into that narrow passageway, over my head, my shoulders, my open hands, washing me in a furious light.

I did not see him sever the head. I only saw him bending over the offering and when he stood up there it was, the eyes unblinking now, and the mouth, which opened twice. Two exhalations without breath, two words without sound, the final benediction. The offering would be gathered up in the square of brown paper and cast into the sea. And my dark, fearful heart brought into the light.

I went into the living room and sat down. I could not stop the tears. Maria had disappeared somewhere in the back where the *babalawo* was washing his hands. I had passed the oval mirror in the holy room just before I had gone back through the beaded curtain to sit down. For a moment I had not recognized my face. I did not recognize the flush on my cheeks, the strange white around my eyes, the wide, dark pupils, my outrageous, extravagant hair. *Asiento. Asiento.* All those months of that long year making the saint – the covered mirrors, the shaved head, the fierce and radiant chastity.

Then they came back into the room and he saw the tears down my face, and took my face in his hands and wiped my tears. "A small sacrifice for such a big thing," he said. "You must come back some day and let me know how it goes."

But I had come so far. How would I ever find my way home? I knew no bridge to take me there.

Authors

Beverly Conner's work has appeared in the collections *Private Voices, Public Lives: Women Writing on the Literary Life* and *Colors of a Different Horse*. She has published short fiction in *Puget Soundings* and was awarded two fellowships at the Hedgebrook Writers Colony. Currently she is at work on her second novel. She teaches creative writing, rhetoric, and literature at the University of Puget Sound.

Hans Ostrom is the author of the novels *Three To Get Ready* (1991) and *Honoring Juanita* (2010), as well as *The Coast Starlight: Collected Poems 1976-2006*. With J. David Macey, he edited *The Greenwood Encyclopedia of African American Literature* (5 volumes). He teaches creative writing, rhetoric, and African American literature at the University of Puget Sound. He is a member of the PEN/American Center.

Ann Putnam teaches creative writing, American literature, and gender studies at the University of Puget Sound. She has published short fiction, personal essays, literary criticism and book reviews in various anthologies such as *Hemingway and Women: Female Critics and the Female Voice* and *Hemingway and the Natural World*, and in journals including the *Hemingway Review*, *Western American Literature*, and the *South Dakota Review*. Her latest publication is the memoir, *Full Moon at Noontide: A Daughter's Last Goodbye* (Southern Methodist University Press).

Acknowledgments

The authors express their gratitude to Ed Putnam; Christopher, Robb, and Courtney Putnam; Terry Conner; Marc and Barbara Conner; Bobbi St. Lazare; Jackie and Spencer Ostrom; Dolen Perkins-Valdez; Barry Bauska; Holly Jones; J. David Macey; Jane Carlin; Sara McIntyre; Hannah Stephenson; William Haltom; Kris Bartanen; Ronald R. Thomas; and the James Dolliver NEH Distinguished Teaching Professorship, University of Puget Sound.

Dedication

To the memory of Esther B. Wagner

CPSIA information can be obtained at www.ICGtesting.com
Printed in the USA
LVOW06s0206140514

385695LV00016B/231/P